Purple Trees

Ursula Wong

Genretarium Publishing ~ Chelmsford, MA

Copyright © 2014 Ursula Sinkewicz

Genretarium Publishing, Chelmsford, MA
www.genretarium.com

For ordering information contact: info@genretarium.com

Cover Images: lassedesignen@123rf.com

and

Nick Verlaan from Pixabay

Cover Design: Jack Simkus

ISBN: 0692207430
ISBN-13:978 0692207437

For more information about the author and her works, go to:

http://ursulawong.wordpress.com

Second printing, October, 2020
3 5 7 9 10 8 6 4 2

To Steve and Steph

The real secrets are not the ones I tell.

—Mason Cooley

ACKNOWLEDGMENTS

A community of writers and readers contributed to *Purple Trees*. In particular, I'd like to thank Kimberly Davis and David Daniel for helping me learn a craft that made this novel possible. I'd like to thank Dale T. Phillips and Vlad Vaslyn for their generosity in editing multiple versions, but also their guidance, encouragement, and moral support. The Tyngsboro Writer's Group, including Joe Ross, Mike Johnson, Bernie Ziegler, Karen Johnson, Brian Hammar, and others, offered comments that made the story significantly better. I'd like to thank my Beta Readers including Mike Gassman, Sue Radak, Pete Ewing, Mike Johnson, Joe Ross, Steph Wong, and Steve Wong for their unvarnished feedback. I'd like to thank David Daniel and Jacquelyn Malone for comments on the final manuscript. I'd like to thank Sharon Bouchard for the diversions and my brother, John Sinkewicz, an honest-to-goodness New England farmer, for technical advice.

I'd like to thank Dale T. Phillips and Genretarium Publishing for having faith when I didn't, and Melinda Phillips.

Finally, I'd like to thank my husband and daughter for their prolific feedback, even though it wasn't always graciously accepted.

Ursula Wong
January, 2014
Chelmsford, Massachusetts

CHAPTER 1

I squinted at the headlights careening through the woods. The car turned onto the long road leading to my cabin and sped up. It was headed toward the big rut. Seeing the car swerve, I gripped the porch railing. The squeal of tires gave way to a sickening thud. Then the car was in the air, arcing toward the stone wall. It landed with a bang and the brutal scrape of metal against rock. When the car stopped moving, its front end was pushed up against the stones, and the driver's side wheel was still spinning. Steam hissed out of the radiator.

The car looked like the one that belonged to my daughter, Claire. A wave of nausea gripped my stomach. Not stopping to put on shoes, I ran to the wreck and wrenched the door open. My granddaughter Angie was inside, clutching the steering wheel.

"Are you hurt?" I asked.

"No, I don't think so."

I helped her climb out of the car. She was barefoot, and in snowflake pajamas. Her face was as white as cream. I put my arm around her trembling shoulders. "What's wrong?"

"Oh, Grandma Lily. Things were out of control. Had to see you."

"Is your mother okay?"

"She doesn't know I'm here. She's with Red." Angie said the name of her mother's boyfriend like it was a bad word.

"Is he why you rushed over?"

"No."

"Claire isn't going to be happy about this." I gestured toward the car.

Angie's eyes were vacant. I led her inside the cabin. She sat by the counter while I made coffee.

"I dreamed about Grandpa Will," said Angie.

I flinched at the mention of my dead husband.

"The dream was so real. I didn't know what to do, so I came here." Angie's hands shook as she filled a spoon with sugar, spilling some on the counter. I wiped it up, put the coffee and cups on a tray, and carried it all into the living room. Angie curled up on the sofa, in front of the fireplace with the smooth, gray stones that stretched up to the ceiling.

I put a match to the kindling in the fireplace. "Tell me about it."

"I was in bed, and someone called my name. I thought it was Red, but then I realized it was Grandpa. I wondered why he was waking me up so early. Then I remembered he's, well, dead. I asked him why he was here. He shook me by the shoulders and told me to leave the house. He told me to run; to save myself."

My stomach tightened. "Red goes into your bedroom?"

"No, Grandma." Angie warmed her hands on the cup of coffee. "Grandpa Will looked terrified. I never saw him look like that. Can I stay with you for a while? I don't want to go home."

"Sure you can stay here, but Claire will have something to say about that."

"I don't care what she says." Angie stared at the fire. "It was just a dream. I'm not like you."

"What do you mean?"

"Ma said you see dead people all the time."

"Your mother says a lot of things." Claire must have told Angie about my conversations with the dead, along with partial truths and falsehoods that no doubt made the story more interesting.

"I don't want to see ghosts. I don't even want to dream about them." Angie brushed a tear from her cheek. "I don't want to be crazy."

"Claire said I was crazy, too?"

Angie nodded.

"I can tell you what happened to me."

"Ma told me everything."

I poked the fire to help it along. "Claire doesn't know squat. She just thinks she does."

I went to the counter that Will had made from a tree he had cut down. He'd sanded and varnished the surface to a glossy finish. I picked up the phone and dialed the only number besides my own that I knew by heart. "Angie's here, and yes, she has your car." At the clatter of Claire's voice, I said, "She'll come home when she's good and ready. You can tell Red that if I see him on my property, I'm hauling out Will's shotgun, and then maybe he'll be your dead boyfriend."

I slammed the receiver down. "Some people know how to hold a grudge." I sat on the sofa. "I don't think it's crazy to dream about the dead. I think a lot of people do it. My mama used to talk to a picture of her daddy after he passed. It made her feel better. I actually saw the people and heard them speak, but it was the same idea."

Angie shivered. I went into the bedroom for the afghan that Will's mother Belle had knitted for me as a Christmas gift one year, with yellow squares trimmed in red and green. I put it over Angie's lap.

"I'm going to tell you things that your mother doesn't know. You may not want to hear some of it, but I kept secrets for a long time, and it caused nothing but grief. This will be the truth. Then you can make up your own mind about everything."

It started in earnest when I was thirteen, a few weeks after Mama died. Her bedroom was off the hallway behind the kitchen, and I was going to her room to sit among her things so I wouldn't feel so lonely. I opened the door and there was someone on the bed. I tiptoed inside, expecting to see Daddy, but it was Mama, with her eyes closed and her hair in corkscrew curls all over the pillow. I ran out of the room and banged the door shut.

After that, I held my breath every time I went past her door.

Then one day when I got home from school, the door to Mama's room was wide open. I yelped like a scared puppy and ran outside. Somebody had opened that door. It wasn't me, and I didn't think it was Daddy, because the last time I saw him anywhere near that room was when they took Mama away, two days before she died.

So Mama's ghost must have opened the door.

Daddy wasn't home, because he had the afternoon shift at the mill that started at three o'clock. He got home around eleven, so I had to get back into the kitchen to make supper for him for when he returned. I was going to make spaghetti and meatballs. I couldn't stand being in the house with Mama's door wide open, let alone being in the kitchen seeing the creepy shreds of wallpaper with dancing spoons, but Daddy had to eat. If I asked Mrs. Baleen from next door to come over and close it, she'd ask why. If I said it was to hide the ghost, she'd blab it all over town.

So I had to take care of this myself.

I stood outside the back door, took three deep breaths, and went in. I ran down the hallway. When I got to Mama's room, I closed my eyes, reached in, and pulled the door shut. Then I ran to the kitchen, opened the junk drawer, and found the key to Mama's door. I raced back down the hallway and put the key in the lock. When it clicked, I felt better. I just hoped that Mama's ghost couldn't walk through walls.

In the next few days, I thought a lot about the ghost in Mama's room. It wasn't like it was going to pick up a knife and kill me, even though Mama was so sick that sometimes she didn't know who I was. If her ghost was in that room, well, it was her room, and she could do what she wanted.

A few weeks later, I decided to go into the room again. There were enough bad feelings in that house already, from Mama's illness and my nightmares. Living with a ghost was too much to bear. I had to go into that room and prove to myself that no one was there. Mama lying on the bed had been a dream, and the wind had pushed the door open. I got the key out of the junk drawer, tiptoed up to Mama's door, and put the key in the lock. My heart was beating so fast I thought I was going to die. I turned the key and opened the door. No one was there. I quickly closed it, locked it, and put the key away.

Later, I asked Daddy if he believed in ghosts. He just smiled. I didn't tell him about Mama, and after he got sick, it didn't seem to matter.

CHAPTER 2

After Mama died, I was free to do whatever I wanted. In the town of Willow Springs, Massachusetts, population two thousand, I could watch the boys play soccer after school, join a club, walk to town, or anything else a 13-year old girl might do in 1964, since I didn't have to rush home to take care of Mama any more. But I was lost, and there was nothing I wanted to do. So every day after school, I went up to my room and watched the cars that passed by the house. I wondered where the people inside were going, and if I'd ever go anywhere. I wondered if anyone would need me again like Mama had. I wondered if I'd live in a big house one day, or whether this place with its sickroom and smoke stains on the ceilings would be the best I'd ever know.

One night, I woke up in the kitchen. I didn't know how I got there. I hated that room. I got a glass of water and went back upstairs. After that, I locked my door at night, so I wouldn't wander the house in my sleep.

Kids at school talked about me. I could tell, because they looked right at me while they covered their mouths so I wouldn't hear. I was different. I didn't have a mother. At least they didn't pick on me, like they did some of the other kids who looked or acted different. I was glad of that. They left me alone, as if they were scared they might catch the disease that would cause their mothers to get sick and die, too.

Daddy said I was spending too much time alone, and that I should go out. He suggested I go to the school dance. I pictured myself in the gym with music blaring, lonely in the crowd. I said okay, as I didn't want Daddy worrying about me. He had to work, so he called Mrs. Ham and asked if she'd give me a ride to the dance. She agreed, and said she was taking her niece, Debbie, who was a year ahead of me. The night of the dance, Daddy told me to have fun. Then he left for work.

Mrs. Ham's car smelled like the inside of a repair shop. She had pink curlers in her hair, and wore a flowery housedress and construction boots. Debbie and I sat in the front seat. We were among the first to arrive at Center School. No one was outside, but the green front door was propped open with a cinder block. When I turned to go up the steps, Debbie grabbed my arm and kept me next to her while her aunt drove away. Then she pulled me down Center Street, past the neat ranch houses.

"Where are we going?" I asked.

"To the cemetery."

"I don't want to go to the cemetery."

"You have to come with me 'cause I don't want to go alone. Cemeteries scare me."

"Then why are we going there?"

"To wait for Jeb."

"Who's Jeb?"

"My boyfriend. We have a date."

I had never been on a date, and dating didn't interest me, but going out with Debbie and her boyfriend might be fun. We went into the drug store, where Debbie bought a pack of gum. Then we went to the cemetery next door and sat on the stone wall with our backs to the headstones. We kicked our feet against the rock, chewed gum, and waited for Jeb. Debbie kept glancing back at the graves.

Soon, we heard the low growl of an engine. Debbie jumped down. "That's him."

A black car with one blue door pulled up next to us. Debbie hopped into the front seat and I got in the back. She slid over to Jeb and kissed him.

I watched them for a while and said, "Ahem."

Debbie turned her head. "You can't come with us."

"I thought we were going on a date."

"You need to go to the dance."

"Aren't you going to drop me off?"

"You can walk, dummy. And you better not say a word about me and Jeb."

"I won't."

"I'll meet you at the dance later."

I stood in the dirt while the car skidded away, with Debbie and Jeb's heads so close together I couldn't tell them apart.

I shuffled up Center Street, past the ranch houses with lights that stared at me like big square eyes. Mr. Franks was standing next to a group of kids outside the school, and pointing at the door. If he saw me, he'd ask who brought me, and why didn't they drop me off at the school. I'd have to make up a story that might get Debbie and me into trouble. I snuck across the lawn to the side of the building, and sat on a rock.

I put my elbows on my knees and swayed to the music coming from the gym. The song brought me back to the only sleepover I had ever gone to, for third-grade girls at Ellie Sim's house. Mama said I should go, even though she wasn't feeling good. Ellie Sim's mother made brownies. Ellie played music on the stereo, and everyone danced. I didn't know how to dance, so I stood at the side. Then Wendy Miller made fun of me because my jeans had a hole at the knee, so I sat on the sofa and talked to a girl named Sandy. Sandy told me a joke. I laughed so hard, I had to grab my belly. Sandy said something else, and I laughed until tears ran down my cheeks. All the girls stared at me. Some giggled and whispered. Later, I couldn't find Sandy, so I asked Ellie where she was. Ellie looked at me funny and said Sandy was her sister who had died two years ago last June.

"Weren't you scared?" Angie's eyes were wide.

"Yes, but when I realized nobody else saw Sandy, I was so embarrassed that I had to leave. I told Mrs. Sims that I was sick, and she called Daddy to come pick me up. I didn't tell Daddy anything. I thought something was wrong with me. Besides, he had enough to worry about already. The next day, Mama moved out of their bedroom upstairs and down to the sickroom behind the kitchen. I pretended Sandy was just a dream."

"Am I going to see ghosts someday too, Grandma?"

"I don't know, Angie."

The moon rose as I sat on that rock at Center School, chewing gum and tapping my feet in time to the song that Ellie Sims had played. I realized with a cold start that Sandy had never been a dream. She was an honest-to-goodness ghost. When I was nine-years old, I had talked to a ghost. Why did Sandy talk to me? What did she want? Why didn't anyone else see her?

That meant I had seen Mama's ghost, too.

I didn't want to be alone in the dark anymore, so I went toward the front of the school, even though Mr. Franks might still be there. Debbie was jogging up the street.

"You didn't go inside?" she asked.

I shrugged.

We melted into a group of kids waiting outside for their rides. When Mrs. Ham drove up, Debbie and I crowded into the front seat.

"How was the dance?" asked Mrs. Ham. She still had curlers in her hair.

"Great," said Debbie. She winked at me.

"Did you have a good time, Lily?"

"It was okay, I guess."

When Daddy came home later that night, I slipped into bed and pretended I was asleep, so I wouldn't have to talk to him. The next day when he asked me about the dance, I said Debbie was mature for her age.

Ghosts became my hobby. I read about them, dreamed about them, and most of all, worried that I would see another one someday. I became a fixture at the library, poring through books, searching for answers. Were ghosts real? How could I keep them away?

I read about daemons, poltergeists, and spirits that moved like shadows. I found very little about ghosts who were like regular people. As time passed, and I didn't see any more ghosts, I tried convincing myself that they were just tricks of my imagination. I missed Mama, and maybe that's why I saw her. Maybe I had seen Sandy's picture somewhere and had imagined her because I was so lonely at the sleepover. Could there be any other explanation?

I kept Mama's door locked anyway.

One Saturday night, Daddy and I were in the living room, watching cowboy shows on TV and eating popcorn. Daddy was in his favorite chair, next to an end table with an oversized ashtray that he kept filling with cigarette butts, no matter how often I emptied it.

"I'm glad you've been doing things after school," he said.

"Huh?"

"Mrs. Ham said she gave you a ride home from the library the other day."

"Oh, yeah."

"Are there any boys in the picture?" Daddy smiled.

My throat tightened. "I dunno."

Daddy lit a cigarette and started to cough. His face turned red.

"Daddy, are you alright?"

"Water," he gasped.

I banged my knee on the coffee table as I got up. I ran to the kitchen and returned with a glass of water. When I handed it to Daddy, there was a drop of blood on his hand.

He managed to take a sip and stop coughing.

"How'd you cut your hand?"

"What are you talking about?"

"There's blood on your hand."

"Don't need a bandage for where that came from, Pumpkin."

Over the next year, Daddy did less work at home, because five days at the mill took all the energy he had. He said that if he did less, he'd be okay. He said as long as he could breathe he'd be fine, because the rest of him was good and strong. I nodded and smiled. He told me I was a good girl. I took care of the lawn in the summer, the leaves in the fall, and shoveled snow in the winter. I cleaned, cooked, and went to school. It was good being busy, but I worried that one day I might become a full-time orphan.

When I was fifteen, Daddy cut his hours at the mill. His boss was pleased, because business was bad. Daddy moved into Mama's old sickroom, because it winded him to climb the stairs. I was so worried about his breathing, I didn't even think about Mama's ghost when he moved downstairs. He sat on the bed and said it was the room where people in our family went to die. I felt bad when he said that, because if he died, I would be all alone. I told him he wasn't going to die, and he said, "Okay, Pumpkin."

9

When I was sixteen, Daddy gave up his job. We didn't know it then, but the mill would close its doors for good by the end of the year. Daddy taught me how to drive in his old Chevy. For practice, we drove through town and along the state road. When Daddy started reading a newspaper in the car, I knew I was doing okay. After I got my license, I took him to all his doctor's appointments. I even took him to Debbie's wedding, when she married Jeb. After the ceremony, Debbie said marriage was great, and that I should try it. I asked her how she knew, because she had only been married for a few hours. She winked at me. They had twins before the year was out. Daddy said it was an unusually short pregnancy.

A few months after the wedding, Daddy said he had a surprise for me. "Joe Halloran from the mill is coming by to take you out."

I stared at him. "You fixed me up?"

"You need to start dating."

"I don't want to go."

"Be a good girl, and do this for me."

I could smell Joe's aftershave all the way upstairs. Daddy's smile faded as he looked at my jeans, sneakers, and t-shirt. Joe looked very clean. We went to Four Rivers for burgers and a movie. Joe said we could go to whatever movie I wanted, so I picked a horror film. Halfway though, Joe put his arm around my shoulders, and I leaned forward. Then the man behind me tapped me on the shoulder and said he couldn't see. I sat back and endured the touch of Joe's arm for the rest of the movie.

When we got home, I mumbled goodnight to Joe and ran into the house, pausing at the foot of the stairs to relax for the first time that evening.

"How'd it go?" asked Daddy. He was in his chair, watching TV.

"Why aren't you in bed?"

"Did you have a good time?"

"Please don't do that again."

"Why? Did Joe try anything?"

"No. Just leave me alone." I started up the steps.

"Lily, you got to promise me something."

"What?"

"You got to marry and have a family. When I'm gone, I don't want you living alone for the rest of your life."

"Why can't you let me do what I want?"

"Be a good girl, and promise me."

"I don't want to."

Daddy started to wheeze.

"Okay, I promise," I said. "But don't fix me up on any more dates."

That night, I dreamed that a man with crooked lips and pinhead eyes was chasing me around the kitchen.

Daddy spent most of his time in bed the winter I turned seventeen. Mrs. Baleen checked in on him during the day while I was at school. When I got home, I fixed supper, cleaned the bedpans, and sat next to the sickbed for a while, just like I had done for Mama.

He had a coughing fit that sent him to the hospital. They hooked him up with oxygen and a tube running into his arm. When he was able to travel, we went all the way into Boston to see a specialist who had performed miracles on others. After examining Daddy, the doctor shook his head. "That's that," said Daddy. He told me he wanted to die at home.

The hospital gave me a canister of oxygen with the yellow paint chipped off in places, and showed me how to use it. They also gave me tubes, a plastic cup, a pink plastic washbasin, and long narrow containers for his pee. I changed the sheets on the bed in Mama's sickroom, and pulled the shades down to make it feel calm.

The room didn't scare me anymore. Daddy's dying did, though.

The ambulance brought him home. The attendants settled him in bed. Daddy said it was good to be back. Then he fell asleep.

When he woke, he mumbled something. I didn't understand, so I asked, "What is it, Daddy?" Then he reached out his hand and suspended it midair. He started to cough, and I thought he was going to die right in front of me. I gave him the oxygen mask. He breathed in and stopped coughing. I heated up some broth and fed him. He took a few sips. I fell asleep in the chair next to the bed.

When I woke up, I knew something had changed. Daddy's eyes were closed, and his cheeks were white. He was smiling. He didn't move, so I went into the kitchen and called the Chief of Police.

"My daddy's dead. What should I do?" I shivered as much from the dancing spoons on the tattered wallpaper as from the corpse in the room down the hall.

I waited on the front porch for the cruiser to arrive. I was cold, but didn't want to go inside for a jacket. Maybe I was hoping Daddy was still alive, and didn't want to see that he wasn't.

Ken Shipman was in the cruiser. There were no flashing lights or sirens. When he wasn't on duty as Chief of Police, Ken worked his business as cattle dealer, finding fresh stock all over New England to sell locally, brokering trades between farmers, and trucking unwanted animals to the slaughterhouse. Occasionally, he'd stop in front of the house and talk to Daddy until the cows banged their hooves inside the cattle truck and raised a commotion with Mrs. Baleen's dogs next door.

I stayed on the front porch while Ken went inside. Another car came by soon afterward, and a man got out carrying a medical bag. He said something to me as he went inside, but I wasn't listening. Then a hearse came. Some men pulled a gurney from the back. After they went into the house, I walked around the car. I hadn't seen a hearse since Mama died, and I wanted to see if it was the same one, but I couldn't tell. They came out carrying Daddy on the gurney, covered in a white sheet. They opened the back of the hearse and slid him inside.

As the hearse drove off, a hand touched my shoulder, and I jumped.

"It's your father, isn't it?" asked Mrs. Baleen from next door. She was wearing a red robe that went all the way down to the ground. "You're going to stay with me tonight."

I shook my head. Ken came over to us.

"You can't be in that house all by yourself," said Mrs. Baleen.

I shook my head again. Then I told Mrs. Baleen I'd come over later if I wanted company.

Ken said I was too young to be alone. I was seventeen and had taken care of sick people all my life, so why didn't they think I could take care of myself?

"Be a good girl, and sleep in my spare room tonight. Then in the morning, you can go home," said Mrs. Baleen.

I followed Mrs. Baleen like a lost puppy, right into her house, and up the stairs to the spare room. I took off my shoes and lay on the bed with my clothes on. I stared out the window, willing it to be morning. When the sky turned the color of a robin's egg, I went home. Mrs. Baleen hadn't gotten up yet.

Later, she came over with a casserole, and asked if I wanted to sleep at her house again that night. I said no thanks. She did the same thing every day for a week, and each time, I took the food and said I wanted to sleep at home. Throughout my life, people brought over casseroles whenever something happened, good or bad. It saved me a lot of cooking, and I eventually grew to like them.

"You still miss him, don't you?" asked Angie. She pulled the afghan up around her shoulders.

I put some wood on the fire. "I think of Will all the time, and Daddy too. That's the way it is with people you love. Just because a person dies, you don't stop loving them."

"You can stop loving a person who's alive, so you can stop loving a person who's dead. I don't see any difference."

"Why would you stop loving a person who's dead?"

"Because they left you."

"You're going to get mad at somebody for dying?"

"Remember Boots, our cat? Ma loved that cat. He used to sleep on her bed. Well, Boots disappeared one day. He used to go into the woods. Ma said some animal probably caught that damn cat. I think Ma's still mad at Boots for going off like that."

"Well that's Claire for you." I took a sip of coffee. "You sleep in my old bedroom upstairs, don't you?"

Angie nodded.

"Does your mother sleep in that downstairs bedroom?"

"No, she sleeps across from me. When Red stays over, they sleep downstairs. Do you think my great-grandma's still in that room?"

I shrugged.

"That house is full of people I don't know about," said Angie.

CHAPTER 3

As I watched Daddy lying in the coffin at the funeral home, it occurred to me that I'd never seen him go so long without a cigarette.

The room smelled of fresh paint. There was nice furniture and curtains on the windows, but without the photos, books, and debris of lives being lived, it was just a room in a funeral parlor.

Daddy's head rested on a ruffled pillow, and his hands were folded over his waist. I kept staring at his chest to see if he was breathing.

I was by myself during most of the wake. There weren't any relatives left, and few friends, as sickness had made us live like hermits. Toward evening, the Baleen family from next door came by. Mrs. Baleen strode in as if she was leading an army, though it was just her husband and the twins.

"Do you need anything, Lily?" she asked.

I said no.

Mr. Baleen knelt next to Daddy, and then came over and shook my hand. The twins stood off to the side, whispering to each other, and pointing at the coffin as if they had never seen a dead body before. Maybe they hadn't.

Mrs. Ham and Debbie came by. Mrs. Ham said she couldn't stay long. Paul, her oldest, was watching the kids, and she had to get back before they wrecked the house.

Ken and Annie Shipman came in with John Stone, Daddy's friend who had a farm on Taylor Road. I didn't know what to say to them, so we just sat.

I went outside after everybody left. It was dark, and the wind was blowing the leaves around. I thought of Daddy, of feeding him and wiping his chin, watching him breathe, and pouring his pee from a canister into the toilet and how sour it smelled. Daddy's cough was so loud it made me jump every time I heard it, even though the sound was as familiar as his voice. I listened for the sound of Daddy's cough in the wind.

The day of the burial, I drove over to the funeral parlor early, in Daddy's rusted-out Chevy. I wanted as much time with him as possible because soon, I would never see him again.

They closed the casket on Daddy at ten o'clock sharp. Ken Shipman, John Stone, and some other men in black suits carried Daddy outside and slid him into the hearse. All of the men were from town, but I didn't think any of them were Daddy's friends except for Ken and John. Then cars lined up behind the hearse, with their engines running. First came the Baleen's beat-up Dodge. Ken and Annie Shipman were in her red car. Mrs. Ham was next, in her dented sedan. John Stone's pickup truck was last in line.

They slid the casket into the hearse, and then added three baskets of flowers that made the air smell sweet. I didn't want anyone to see me cry, so I started down the driveway on foot, toward Brook View Cemetery next door. I counted my steps, because it gave me something to do.

Before I got to the road, the funeral director ran up behind me. "Where are you going?" he asked. He was out of breath, and his face was red.

"To the grave," I said.

"Please get in the car." He signaled for the hearse, which came down the driveway and stopped beside us.

I didn't want to be in a car full of strange men, but I'd been taught to always be a good girl, so I got in.

We crossed the road, turned almost right away, and went in through the iron gate of the cemetery. We drove up the hill and parked on the grass. We went so slow, I could have got there faster if I had kept walking.

They carried the casket from the car to a hole in the ground. There was a pile of dirt next to it, covered with a ratty green carpet. I thought it would have looked better if they had used a carpet in a different color, like orange or purple.

Mama's grave was the next one over. I touched her headstone. I had spent the day of her funeral pretending it was someone else in her coffin. I remembered very little of her burial, just an intense sadness.

On the other side of the green carpet, cemetery workers in overalls leaned on their shovels. The funeral director asked me if I wanted to say a few words. I said no. He called for a silent prayer and then touched my elbow. I jerked it away.

"It's time to leave," he said.

"I'm staying."

He walked to the hearse and stood next to it, looking like he was mad that he had to wait. The rest of us watched as the workers lowered the casket into the grave. They started shoveling in the dirt, which made a thud when it landed on Daddy. On the third thud, I ran across the graves to the parking lot at the funeral parlor, jumped into Daddy's car, and drove home.

That night, I found a pack of Daddy's cigarettes tucked in the pocket on the side of his lounge chair. I took them outside, sat on the front steps, and lit one to smell his scent. I knew the smoking had killed him, but I didn't care. I talked to the memory of him and felt better.

I told Daddy I hoped he was okay, wherever he was.

I took a puff of the cigarette and coughed. Then I asked him if he was with Mama, and to say hi for me.

I closed my eyes and pictured him in the living room, sitting in his chair, a cigarette squeezed between his thumb and index finger. I saw the colors of the room: the white curtains, green walls, the plaid sofa, his brown chair, and the curlicue of gray smoke rising from the cigarette.

I thought about my future while I sat on those steps. I remembered my promise to Daddy that someday I would marry. I tried to picture the man he would want me to marry, but I sensed him more than saw him. He would be kind. He would protect me. Daddy was too sad to protect me. I wanted to live in a big white house and wear nice clothes. I wanted to go to parties at Mrs. Bishop's magnificent home with eight chimneys and black shutters on the windows. I would sip punch, eat cake, and discuss the news with people who mattered. Most of all, I didn't want to be lonely.

I sat there for hours, until the sound of a car speeding down the road brought me out of the daydream. If it wasn't for that car, I might still be sitting there.

"You just pictured your daddy in your head," said Angie. "You talked to him, but he didn't say anything. You're right. Ma didn't know what she was talking about. She said you saw ghosts all the time."

I got up and put another piece of wood on the fire. The sparks flew upwards in a display of miniature fireworks.

"Okay. I'll make breakfast and drive you home."

"I don't want to go home."

"Then we'll just swing by your house to pick up some clothes, and I'll drive you to school."

"I'm not going to school."

"You have to go to school."

"Ma didn't."

"She ended up waitressing at the Mill Rat. Is that what you want?"

Angie sighed. "I'd like eggs and toast, please."

"Are you going to school?"

"Not today, Grandma. Please?"

I nodded. Angie looked like she needed a day off. Everybody does now and then. I took her by the hand, and we went into the kitchen. I made cheese omelets and toast. When we finished eating, we went back to the living room with a fresh pot of coffee.

CHAPTER 4

One night when I was little, I was asleep in bed when a noise woke me up. It sounded like somebody was in the kitchen, hitting the walls. I wanted to hide under my bed, but I went to get Daddy. I peeked into their room. He wasn't there. Mama wasn't there either, because she was in the hospital. I crept down the stairs and looked into the kitchen from the shadows, expecting to see burglars ransacking the house. Daddy was tearing a sheet of wallpaper down with his bare hands. The jagged edge left at the bottom looked like a mountain range. He worked like a madman, running from wall to wall, pulling and scratching at that wallpaper. The back of his shirt was wet and his forehead shiny with sweat. When he finally stopped, tattered pieces remained on the walls where the paper wouldn't tear off. I melted into the dark as he walked past me and up the stairs.

The wallpaper had pictures of spoons the color of caramel candy, on a background of sunshine yellow. The spoons had little arms and legs that were in the middle of a kick or a jump, and they were dancing all over that paper. Mama had picked it out just before she went into the hospital for the first time. She said the dancing spoons made her laugh. Daddy was going to surprise her by having it up when she got home, and he did, but she was too sick to enjoy it.

I hated that wallpaper. I was glad when he ripped it down. I wanted to help him, but I didn't. Daddy didn't know how much I hated that wallpaper, and I couldn't tell him, because Mama had liked it.

As I wandered through the house the morning after Daddy's funeral, everything reminded me of my parents: the white plate with shamrocks, the matching vases by the front window, and their wedding picture hanging in the hallway that led to Mama's bedroom downstairs. I felt like I was trespassing in my own home.

We never touched those walls after the night Daddy had torn the wallpaper down. A chill hit my spine every time I passed a scrap of paper with a picture of one of those stupid spoons. I tried not to look, but my eyes went to them anyway. I asked Daddy if we should clean up those walls. He said no. It was as though he needed to see the damage.

The day after the funeral, I went into the garage and found a can of white paint, a roller, a brush, a paint tray, and a paint scraper. My hands shook, but I scraped the remaining paper off the kitchen walls. Age had made the pattern barely recognizable, but I knew what it was. I swept up the bits from the floor and dumped them into the trashcan outside.

Then, I painted. Drips fell onto the baseboards, floor, and stove, but I didn't care. The walls were white, and the dancing spoons were gone forever. That night I dreamed that the dancing spoons were chasing me, and I woke up screaming.

I hadn't gone through the mail since they had taken Daddy away, and it was starting to pile up. Every day I collected it from the box at the end of the driveway and threw it on top of the bureau by the front door. When letters started spilling onto the floor, I tossed everything into a brown paper bag and took it out to the front steps.

There were fliers from the grocery store in Willow Springs, several issues of the local newspaper, a sympathy card with a check inside for five dollars, and a letter from the town containing the property tax bill.

Daddy hadn't paid the taxes since Mama died.

After I paid for the funeral, there was little money left, and nowhere near enough to pay the tax bill. If I sold the house, I wouldn't have a place to live. I could ask Mrs. Ham for money, but I knew she didn't have any. I had to quit school and get a job. School was nothing more than a place to go every day, so I didn't mind quitting. But who would hire me, and what would I do? What if I couldn't find a job? What if the town took the house and kicked me out? I would end up living in a shack out in the woods.

I sat on the front steps holding the tax bill in my hand, hoping the wind would whisk it away.

I went inside and phoned Ken Shipman.

In a shaky voice, I told him that I needed to find a job.

He asked if I was okay.

"Taxes are due, and I got to find work," I said.

"Annie and I can loan you the money, Lil."

"Thanks, but I really need a job."

"Well, they always need second shift waitresses at the Mill Rat, you know, the Mill Restaurant, but that's a tough job because you have to deal with the drunks. I think they need somebody to help in the office at the Co-Op, too."

I thanked Ken and hung up. It might not be so bad working in a garden and farm supply store. If they didn't hire me in the office, maybe they'd let me stack supplies in the warehouse.

The next morning, I put on the dress I had worn to the funeral, combed my hair, and got into Daddy's Chevy. I drove past the train depot where the grain sheds were, through the center of town, and along the state road to the Co-Op.

I opened the door to the store and almost gagged at the smell. It was a cross between ammonia, grass, and I didn't know what else. I had never smelled anything so vile. I spoke to Bruce Davis, the manager, and, as politely as I could, asked him what that smell was.

"Fertilizer," he said. "Don't worry, you'll get used to it. And it's seasonal. We don't carry it all year." Bruce was bald and wore a white belt, black pants, and a plaid shirt. He asked me if I could type. I said a little, from taking secretarial classes at the high school.

Then I met Peggy Lynn who looked me up and down, and said, "She'll do." Bruce said he'd see me on Monday morning at seven o'clock sharp, and he'd show me how to open the store.

Even though the smell of the fertilizer bothered me, I was relieved to have a job. On the way home, I stopped in town and bought myself a candy bar to celebrate. By the time I got to the house, I was wondering how many paychecks I would get before Bruce and Peggy realized I couldn't do anything, and fired me.

But within a week, I had settled in at the Co-Op. I opened the store in the mornings and stepped inside to that smell of fertilizer, grass seed, and a thousand other things. I did get used to the smell, but it took some time. Each day brought something different: a new face, a problem with a bill, or a rush order. I never knew what to expect, and I liked that. Best of all was the relief of having money coming in that I could use to pay the tax bill.

I worked behind a counter separating the office area from the rest of the store. The office had two chairs with cracked leather seats, four filing cabinets, two desks, a phone, and an adding machine. One section of the store had nothing but garden supplies, including seeds, hoes, rakes, water hoses, and potting soil, although the farmers thought it was funny that anyone would pay for dirt. Another area had horse equipment, both new and used, ointments, brushes, and coffee mugs with pictures of foals. The shelves in the back were overloaded with things for cows. There were boxes of mastitis treatment and other medicines, hoses, milk filters, balm, stainless steel pails, and calendars with scenes of cows in fields of clover.

I worked with Peggy, who was bookkeeper and a self-proclaimed relationship expert. She had six kids, each with a different father. Two of the boys still lived with her, in a trailer on a crescent of grass tucked in between the road and the woods, near the town line. Peggy's face, arms, and legs were lean, but her torso had the general shape of a beer can. At four feet, ten inches tall, she wore high heels and short skirts with religious regularity. Her dark hair hung down to her shoulders. She had thick bangs and wore black-rimmed glasses.

One day, Peggy asked if I would go with her to the courthouse on Saturday afternoon. I said I would, and then asked why. Peggy said she was getting married. Her expression was so deadpan, I thought it was a joke.

"Who are you going to marry?" I asked.

"Fidelio."

"Who?"

Peggy said she met Fidelio a week ago at a local bar called the Snake Pit. He needed to get married so he could stay in the country. Otherwise, he was going to be deported.

"He was so beautiful, I wanted to cry," said Peggy. After a few drinks, she said she'd help out and marry him. Fidelio made the arrangements, they had blood tests, and the final step was on Saturday, for the ceremony and signing of the marriage certificate.

"But you hardly know him," I said.

"What's there to know?" asked Peggy. "Besides, I've never been married before, and I want to find out what it's like." She paused. "Please come. I don't have a lot of girlfriends."

That night, as I ate a bologna sandwich and drank a soda out on the front steps, I pictured Peggy in a long white dress, holding a bouquet of roses, posing at the door of the Unitarian Church. She would smile like a virginal bride, toss the bouquet, and I would catch it.

Peggy's actual wedding was in a small room in the basement of the town hall. Instead of a long white dress, Peggy wore a yellow miniskirt, and a hat with a blue feather. Fidelio came in jeans and a red flannel shirt. The Justice of the Peace shook hands with Peggy and Fidelio, positioned them under the American flag, and spoke in a solemn voice. After each one said, "I do," we signed the marriage certificate, and it was done.

Peggy grabbed Fidelio's arm, and we headed across the common toward the Snake Pit to celebrate. The feather on Peggy's hat came up to Fidelio's chin, and it waved like a wispy hand as they walked. The bar was horseshoe-shaped, and it glowed like honey. The room was full of dust, smoke, and a feeling of expectation. Country music played on the jukebox. A couple hugged on the dance floor.

Peggy sat between Fidelio and me. She ordered three margaritas.

It was my first time in a bar. Daddy had smoked like a fiend, but he never drank, and I had never tasted liquor before. The margarita was light green, and came in a stemmed glass rimmed in white crystals. I put a few grains on my tongue and then brushed it all off. I didn't care much for salt. I took a sip. It tasted like turpentine cut with sweet lime juice.

Peggy said, "Good, huh?"

I asked the bartender for a glass of water.

As Peggy tried to get the bartender's attention for another round, Fidelio got to his feet.

"Gotta go," he said.

"What?" asked Peggy.

"I'm meeting some friends."

"Let me pay the bill, and I'll go with you."

"No, you stay here." He took a few steps toward the door and then came back. "If you ever need anything, give me a call." Then he left.

Peggy ordered a shot of tequila.

"He wouldn't even kiss me. Did you notice? And I'm his wife," Peggy said. "The worst of it is I should know how to keep a man, 'cause I had enough of 'em. Marriage ain't what it's cracked up to be." Peggy drank the tequila in one gulp. "I even bought new sheets." She smiled, showing dark spaces where her back teeth should have been. Peggy ordered another shot. I nursed my drink.

I drove Peggy to her trailer later that evening. She climbed the front steps and stumbled backwards. I opened the door and pushed her inside. The kitchen was narrow, cramped, and very brown. I yelled hello, but no one answered. There wasn't enough space to walk side-by-side down the hall, so I leaned Peggy against the wall and slid her toward the bedroom. I put her on the bed, took off her shoes and hat, covered her with a blanket, and drove home.

As I lay in bed, I didn't know what to make of Peggy. She was smart enough to raise a bunch of kids and support them by herself. She owned that little trailer and probably had a few bucks in the bank. She thought she knew everything there was to know about men, and probably did, but things just didn't seem to work out for her.

Maybe Peggy was unlucky. I wondered if I was unlucky, too.

On Monday, Peggy was in the office, acting as though nothing had happened. I wanted to ask if she had seen Fidelio since Saturday, but instead, I got a cup of coffee and answered the phone.

That night, I went out on the front steps, lit a cigarette, and waited to relax. "I miss you, Daddy," I said. The wind carried my words away. I closed my eyes and thought of him. When I opened them, a man was sitting next to me who looked just like Daddy, and he was wearing a blue suit just like the one Daddy had on in the coffin.

I yelped like a scared dog. A chill shook me. I jumped to my feet, ran into the house, and slammed the door. Whoever was sitting there on the porch reminded me of Daddy, but Daddy was dead and buried. Who would want to scare me like that? I turned the lock and leaned with my back against the door.

It took a few minutes for me to calm down. I must have just imagined seeing Daddy because he was on my mind. Unless there was a shovel tucked inside that coffin, there was no way he could get out of the grave. Maybe it was his ghost. I shivered again. I didn't like ghosts, and didn't want any hanging around the house. I thought of Mama's ghost. Maybe this place was turning into a haunted house.

Besides, I was grown up and working for a living. Grownups don't believe in ghosts. I crept to the window and peeked outside. No one was on the steps or in front of the house. I checked that the back door was locked. I grabbed the key from the junk drawer and locked the door to the sickroom, just in case.

I didn't go out on the front steps the next night, or the next. I was afraid of what I might see. By Friday night, I wanted the smoke that reminded me of Daddy, so I marched outside, sat down, and lit up.

On the second puff, Daddy showed up.

I jumped to my feet. "Who the hell are you?"

"It's just me, honey."

"Are you a ghost?"

"It's Daddy."

"My daddy's under six feet of dirt in Brook View Cemetery." My heart was racing, but I wasn't going to let this ghost get the best of me, even if it was Daddy.

"Don't be scared."

"How do I know it's you?"

"Ask me something."

"What's the name of my favorite doll?" I pictured my doll's long brown hair and eyes that closed when she lay down. I loved that doll. The figure next to me on the porch seemed to be thinking. He was a little fuzzy around the edges, but he sure looked like Daddy. I got ready to run.

"Liza," he said.

I sat down. It really was Daddy, back from the dead. I asked him how he was doing, and if he ever saw Mama. He didn't say anything. I took a long drag to calm down. I turned my head to the side to breathe out, because I didn't want to blow smoke into Daddy's face. When I looked back, he was gone.

At first, Daddy visited me every few days. After a week or so, he came whenever I lit up. It was good seeing him. I wasn't so lonely when he was there.

Before long, I had smoked all of Daddy's cigarettes. I liked smoking by then. I didn't want anyone to know about my new habit, so I drove all the way to Four Rivers one night to buy some more. I walked up and down the aisles of the grocery store to see if anyone knew me. Then I got in line behind a lady who was buying a loaf of bread, a carton of milk, and a package of breakfast sausages. By the time it was my turn, I had convinced myself that the cashier was going to refuse to sell me cigarettes because I was too young. I wanted to run, but I needed those smokes.

"Cigarettes, please," I said.

The cashier mumbled something.

Oh no, I thought. She's not going to give me any. "They're for my daddy."

"I don't care who they're for, what kind do you want?" She had a long nose and blue glasses decorated with rhinestones.

I thought they were all the same, so I pointed to a package that looked like Daddy's brand. I handed her a dollar. She gave me a pack of cigarettes and change. I walked to the car without looking back, and then drove down the road to a little park. I sat in the car and lit up to calm down.

The cigarettes cost more than a gallon of gas and less than a dozen eggs. I gave up eggs so I could afford the cigarettes. I didn't think it was much of a sacrifice. After all, when I smoked, I got to see Daddy.

CHAPTER 5

"I hadn't thought about Grandpa Will for days, and then all of a sudden he was in my dream. He seemed so real," said Angie. She stood up and walked to the fireplace.

"He came to you for a reason."

"What could it be?"

"Has Red been bothering you?" I asked.

Angie turned and stared at me. "I told you, everything's fine. I don't want to talk about him."

I had bumped into Ken Shipman at the post office awhile back, and we started talking about Red. I told Ken that Red was originally from upstate New York and came to Willow Springs a few years ago. Ken said Red had already been through a couple of jobs. Once in a while, he spent the night sobering up in jail. Ken had seen him with different women, and recently at the Snake Pit with the new secretary from the office at the lumberyard. By then, Red was already dating Claire. I wanted to tell Claire that Red was no good, but she'd never listen to me.

"Then tell me what's going on with your mother."

"Why do you want to talk about her?"

"Please?"

"I always have to prove myself." Angie sat down and crossed her legs.

"Me, too."

"Ma usually works two shifts, 'cause we need the money." Angie chewed a fingernail. "She's going to kill me when she sees her car on that rock."

"I'll handle her."

"I make supper when I get home from school, so Ma and I can eat together before she heads out for second shift. One afternoon, I put a chicken on the stove to *boil and went to my room to do homework. I forgot about the chicken, and it burnt. I was cutting off the black part, trying to save some of it, when Ma came in. She started yelling at me, saying I was useless and couldn't do anything right. I didn't burn that chicken on purpose, Grandma. Ma didn't talk to me for days."*

"Claire has held a grudge against me for twenty years, and no matter what I do, I can't make it up to her. I wish she'd lighten up a little, at least with you."

"I played a trick on her once."

"Oh?"

"It was Easter, and I was dyeing eggs. On a whim, I dyed a raw egg light blue, which was Ma's favorite color, and put it in the basket next to the hard-boiled eggs. On Easter morning, she came down to the kitchen for breakfast. I gave her some coffee, a slice of fresh bread, and handed her the basket of eggs."

"Ma sipped some coffee, asked for an aspirin, and said she had to stop going to the Snake Pit. Then she picked up the light blue egg and was about to crack it against the table. I asked her if she wouldn't rather have the yellow egg. Ma accused me of doing something to the yellow egg. I just said she'd be happier with it."

"Then Ma said, 'You can't fool me. I'm sticking with this blue one.'"

"Ma smashed the egg against the table to crack it. The insides spewed out all over her plate, the bread, and her hand. I laughed."

"What did Claire do?"

"She didn't talk to me for the rest of the day."

"That's my girl. Say, where does Red go when your mother's at work?"

"With her. If he comes over early, she eats with him. I take a plate into my room and eat alone. Then they go to the Mill Rat together, and he waits for her at the bar."

One Friday after work, Peggy suggested we go to the Snake Pit for a drink. We sat at a table where we had a good view of the bar. I ordered a soda. Peggy ordered beer and a shot of whiskey. As we waited for our drinks, Peggy pointed out a man at the bar with shiny black hair and wearing workman's clothes.

"That's Sam Wheeler," Peggy said. "He's got a place on North Road, and works as a mechanic at Pip's Garage. He lived with his parents until they died. Never been married." Peggy took a sip of beer. "He wants me bad, but I won't go out with him."

"Why?" I asked.

"Because I'm a hot ticket," said Peggy.

"No, why won't you go out with him?"

"Never seen him sober."

"He must be sober sometimes, to hold down a job."

"You'd be surprised," said Peggy. She drank the shot of whiskey in one gulp.

Sam was sitting with his head down, staring at his drink. He looked up and turned to Peggy. It was as if he knew we were talking about him. He came over to our table.

"Hey, Peggy," said Sam. He stood with one hand on his hip, and the other holding a bottle of beer. He was very tall.

"Hey, Sam."

"You gonna invite me to sit down?"

"Do what you like," said Peggy.

"Who's this?" Sam asked, as he nodded at me. He pulled a chair out with his foot and sat down.

Peggy told him my name and said I lived a mile from town, out by the train depot.

"I know the place," he said. He winked at Peggy.

"I ain't going out with you Sam, so don't even ask," said Peggy.

"Maybe Lily wants to go out with me."

I didn't say anything.

"She's too young for you."

"We'll see about that." Sam got up and went back to the bar. A moment later, another round of drinks came to our table. We looked at Sam, who nodded and turned back to his beer.

Later that night, I woke to a pounding noise at the front door. I tiptoed downstairs in the dark and peeked out the window. Sam Wheeler was standing on the porch.

"Lily, you in there?"

I held my breath.

"If you're in there Lily, open the door."

Maybe he needed something. Maybe it was an emergency. I opened the door a crack. "What do you want?"

"I need to talk to you."

His breath smelled bad.

"Is something wrong?"

He pushed past me into the living room. I clutched the neck of my nightgown and realized how stupid I was to have opened the door.

"I like you, Lily. I like you a lot."

"I have a boyfriend," I lied. My hands were shaking.

Sam swayed as he stood. He stepped toward me. "I bet he can't kiss you like this." Sam grabbed me. In an instant, his lips were on mine. His tongue was inside my mouth. A pain flashed through my head along with the image of a face from a nightmare I had as a little girl. The face had crooked lips, white hair, a swollen nose, and pinhead eyes. I jumped and clamped my teeth down.

Sam stepped back and put his hand over his mouth. "What you bite me for?"

"Go home," I yelled.

"You could have just asked me to leave. You didn't have to bite me. I know when I ain't wanted."

Sam walked out the door. I locked it and went to the window. His truck backed down the driveway too fast and then sped off.

I lay awake, expecting Sam to come back, but he didn't. Eventually, I fell into a restless sleep. When I woke up, I made a pot of coffee and called Peggy.

After I told her about Sam Wheeler's midnight visit, I asked if I should call Ken Shipman at the Sheriff's Office and file a complaint.

"Don't do that, honey," said Peggy. "Ken will follow him like a hound dog. The poor man might lose his job."

"But he attacked me."

"He didn't attack you. He just kissed you. Don't you know the difference? You can bet your next paycheck he'll be in church on Sunday. He may be a drunk, but he's harmless."

"What if he comes back?"

"I'll talk to him. Don't worry."

I hung up wondering about the face with crooked lips that I had pictured when Sam had his tongue in my mouth.

"Somebody I didn't like tried to kiss me once," said Angie. She twirled a lock of raven hair around her finger. "It gave me the creeps."

"Who was it?" I expected Angie to say it was Red, and I was ready to grab the shotgun from the front closet and go find the bastard. I took a breath and waited.

"I was in second grade. A boy watched me all the time. I thought he was trying to copy my schoolwork. One day I was by myself at recess, because I didn't

feel like playing baseball with the other girls. I was sitting on the swings, watching them choose sides. He came over and leaned toward me with his mouth open."

"What did you do?"

"Ran away."

I laughed and Angie smiled.

It snowed buckets that winter, with one nor'easter after another. It seemed that all I did was shovel the driveway, go to work, and occasionally go out with Peggy. We avoided the Snake Pit. I think she felt bad about introducing me to Sam, but he didn't come by the house all winter. I told her I didn't want to meet anyone else. She asked me if I was planning to spend the rest of my life alone. I almost told her about Daddy, but I didn't think she would understand.

At home, the kitchen walls churned with those dancing spoons. Even though I couldn't see them under the paint, it still felt like they were there. I unlocked the door to the sickroom and Mama's ghost. I even went inside a few times to tell her Daddy was around, but I never saw her.

On snowy weekends, I curled up in Daddy's chair in the living room, lit a cigarette, and waited for him. He came by more often as the snow grew deeper. I asked him if he knew anyone with white hair and crooked lips. He said no. We watched TV and smoked cigarettes. I almost told him about Sam Wheeler, but I didn't want to worry him. I didn't tell him about my nightmares. After all, they were just silly dreams, but how could they be so specific, always about that face and the kitchen?

When Daddy was with me, everything in the house seemed normal.

Finally, the snow melted, and the trees bloomed like big overgrown flowers, in the glory that was spring in New England. I took walks in the woods behind the house as the weather got warm, and even planned a garden, so I'd have something to do in the evenings.

On one particularly beautiful day, I was at my desk at the Co-Op, when the bell clanged as the door opened. The handsomest man I had ever seen strode into the store, smiling like he was pleased with the general state of humanity. He wore a red baseball cap, and a black t-shirt dotted with bits of hay. He had a ruddy complexion. His eyes scanned the room as he came up to the counter.

When he looked at me, my face got hot, and I turned back to my work. Peggy nudged me with her elbow. I stood up and went over to the counter. He introduced himself.

"So you're Will Phelps," I said. "I've taken your orders before over the phone."

"I had to go to town today, so I thought I'd stop in for a change."

Will said he had a farm on the other side of Willow Springs, next to John Stone's place.

I told him John was an old friend of my daddy's.

"Well ain't that interesting." Will leaned on the counter with one elbow. "Cows broke through the fence, so I need some barbed wire. While you're at it, gimme a few rolls of baler twine. Oh, and don't forget my discount." He winked at me.

"Discount?"

"Boss gives me ten percent."

"I don't know about any discounts."

"Go ask the boss."

"He ain't here."

"Well where is he?"

"How would I know?"

"When will he be back?"

"I don't know."

He winked again.

If I gave Will Phelps the discount, and it was a mistake, it might be taken out of my pay. I started to sweat.

I turned to Peggy, who smiled but turned away. I took the pen in my hand and wrote little circles in the air. I didn't know what to do, so I calculated ten percent, subtracted it from the total, and handed the bill to Will.

"Sign, please. Drive around back to the warehouse to pick up your supplies."

"Yeah, I know." Will signed the bill, smiled at me, and walked out. The bell rang as the door slammed shut.

I turned toward Peggy. "Thanks a lot for helping me."

"He asks for a discount every time he comes into the store. You're the first to give him one." Peggy chuckled as she turned back to her work.

My heart sank. Will Phelps was a vulture. He'd steal money from a poor, innocent girl? I hoped he crashed his truck into a tree on the way to his stinking farm. What kind of friend was Peggy? I stuck my tongue out at her back.

I looked at the copy of the bill to check my new debt. Will had crossed out the ten percent, circled the full amount of the bill, and signed it.

I asked Peggy how old he was.

"I would guess thirty-five, give or take," said Peggy.

Sixteen from the way he acted, I thought.

The essence of Will stayed with me for the rest of the day. I kept thinking about the expression on his face and the color of his eyes. He was just a farmer though, and wouldn't have much money, but he sure was good looking.

Next time he ordered supplies, I might add a little extra to his bill to see how he liked it. I wondered how his kiss would feel. I wouldn't let myself think about anything more than that.

A few days later, Will stopped by the Co-Op again.

"You ain't getting a discount, so don't even ask," I said.

"You can't blame a man for having some fun."

"Why don't you go have fun someplace else?"

"Let me make it up to you. How about having supper with me tonight?"

I looked at Peggy, who had turned her chair around to face us.

"You want to take me out?" I asked.

"I do."

"Where?"

"How about the Mill Rat?"

After he left, Peggy said, "Don't give it away too fast, but wear something short."

I changed clothes three times before settling on the red skirt and pink satin blouse I had bought from Laura's Dress Store in town, along with a few other things for work. I couldn't afford much, so I shopped from the discount racks. As I looked at myself in the mirror, I thought Peggy would approve. Then it occurred to me that satisfying Peggy's tastes might not be the best thing. I heard a knock on the door, grabbed my sweater, and ran downstairs.

Will was waiting outside, looking scrubbed clean. His hair was slicked back and shiny. I thought he didn't look natural without his baseball cap. He put his hand on my back as we went down the porch steps. I arched away from his touch. I didn't know what girls did on dates, except what Peggy told me. She said she always kissed on first dates, but I shouldn't let him get to second base just yet. I was too embarrassed to say I didn't know what that meant.

I wanted Will to think I was interested, so I sat near him in the pickup truck, but not so close that we were touching in any way.

I remembered Sam Wheeler's nighttime visit and asked Will if he drank. Will said he did, but not when he was working with heavy machinery or taking care of the cows, which was all the time.

The Mill Rat, also known as the Mill Restaurant, was on the lower road to town, near the river. There was a big sign across the road with bullet holes in it, declaring it the *Best Restaurant Around*. When the woolen mill was operating, the Mill Rat was the place to go for food and drink before, during, and after work. After the mill closed, the restaurant survived, due to loyal clientele and cheap weekend specials. I'd heard the food wasn't always delicious, but the portions were big.

We sat at a table covered in a sheet of red plastic, and Will ordered two beers. We ate steak with sides of spaghetti and peas, by the light of a candle stuck in an empty Chianti bottle. I barely touched my beer, so when we finished eating, Will drank the rest of it.

Over pie and coffee, he asked me to tell him my life story. He rested his chin on his hand and looked at me through half-closed eyes, but somehow he seemed interested in what I was saying. I told him about Mama dying and then Daddy. I told him how I had to quit school and go to work to pay off the taxes.

As Will drove me home, we didn't talk much. He followed me up the steps to the front door. He put his hands on my back and pulled me close. Visions of Sam Wheeler's tongue flashed through my head, and I cringed as I stared at Will's chest. His lips brushed my neck, and he let me go. He said good night, walked to the truck, and drove off.

I went inside and locked the door, relieved by Will's gentleness, but fearful of what might happen the next time he brought me home from a date. Touching would eventually lead to sex, and I didn't want to sleep with him or anyone. I had never understood why girls in school expected sex to be wonderful. The thought of it made me cold and fearful. No one had told me it would be awful. I just knew.

What would Will do if I didn't let him kiss me, or touch me anymore? Would he walk away mad? Would he force himself on me?

I was poor, uneducated, in debt, and all I had going for me were my looks. I didn't want to lose him because of sex. There weren't a lot of men to choose from in Willow Springs. Most kids got married right after high school. Those who didn't usually found a job, lived at home, and spent weekend nights drinking at the Snake Pit, just like Sam Wheeler.

Will seemed different.

The next day at the Co-Op, Peggy wanted me to tell her everything that happened on my date. I didn't. I figured anything that went on between Will and me was our business, not hers. Besides, he hadn't asked me out again, and there wasn't much to tell.

I didn't see Will for a week. I was at work when I looked out the window at the rain, and saw him running from his truck to the store. When he got inside, he took off his hat and shook off the water.

"Hi Lil," he said.

I took my time going over to the counter.

"Can I help you with something?" I drummed my fingers on the wood.

"You mad at me?" he asked.

"I haven't seen you all week, and you haven't bothered to call, so why should I be mad?"

"You know a farmer has to take advantage of good weather in the summer to get the haying done."

"Oh."

"Let me take you to supper."

My lips said yes before my head could make up its mind.

That night, after eating Yankee pot roast at the Mill Rat, Will kissed me as we stood on the porch. Then he put his arms around me. I wanted to squirm away, but I had made up my mind that Will was probably the best I would find in Willow Springs, so I stood there and took it. I kept telling myself it wasn't so bad.

I watched from the window as he drove away. Then I went into Mama's sickroom. I didn't see her on the bed, so I put on her blue terrycloth robe, and slipped my feet into her fuzzy slippers. I went outside to the front steps and lit a cigarette. The darkness felt like a friend. I could see a light in Mrs. Baleen's kitchen window. Daddy showed up on the fourth puff.

I told Daddy that I met the man who owned the place next to John Stone. I explained that Will had acreage and cows. I said that if I married Will, I would become a woman of means. I would live in a big white farmhouse with elegant furniture and a kitchen that was so clean a person could eat off the floor. Mrs. Bishop would be impressed, and invite me to tea in her mansion. We'd talk about her ancestors who came over on the Mayflower. Daddy smiled.

"You talking to somebody?" The sound of Mrs. Baleen's voice hit me like a splash of cold water. If she saw Daddy, she'd tell everyone in town that I had a ghost at the house. I swatted the smoke.

"I talk to myself sometimes, too," she said. "I didn't know you smoked."

"Once in a while. It helps my digestion." I turned toward Daddy. He wasn't there. I offered Mrs. Baleen a cigarette.

"No, thanks," she said. "How they treating you down the Co-Op?"

"Do you still see Mrs. Baleen?" asked Angie.

"I drop by her house once in a while. She was a good neighbor, helping when Daddy was sick, and then checking in on me after he died. We never became close friends, though. We just didn't have that much in common."

"Just like you don't have much in common with Red," Angie said with a smirk.

"He drinks too much and can't hold down a job. I don't know what Claire sees in him."

"You think he's a bum."

"Maybe I do."

"I liked him at first. I asked him why everybody called him Red. He said it was because of his hair, and I laughed, because he's as bald as an egg. When he first started coming around, I was glad Ma was going out and having some fun for a change. I used to wait up for her. Then one night, she didn't come home until morning. I asked her where she was, and why didn't she call. She said they stayed up talking, and lost track of time. She said I shouldn't wait up any more. Then

Red *started spending the night, and he turned mean, calling me Fat Girl when Ma wasn't around."*

"Does he spend every night at your house?"

"No. Sometimes Ma stays at his place in town, but they're not together every night."

"Nobody waited up for me when I met Will. Mama and Daddy were already gone."

Angie sighed and put her head on my shoulder.

"First time I met Red, I came by your house just before supper with a bushel of apples for your mother."

"I remember."

"Claire and Red were having a beer in the kitchen. Red asked me to sit down and offered me a drink. Your mother said I couldn't stay, so I sat down. Then you came in. For a split second, Red looked at you like a hungry man looks at fresh meat. But I thought that couldn't be. Claire would never go out with a man like that."

"You really thought that?"

"Is there something you want to tell me?"

Angie crossed her arms. "You said Ma would never go out with anyone like that."

"Claire's a good woman, honey. But I know for a fact that love can blind a person."

"Can we talk about something else?"

I saw a lot of Will after that. We went out to eat and took a ride, or went out for a beer. One night we went to the Snake Pit. Sam Wheeler was sitting at the bar.

Will and I went to a table.

Sam Wheeler came over. "This your boyfriend?"

"I guess so," I said.

Will winked at me.

Sam Wheeler turned to Will and said, "Watch out for her, she bites." Sam turned and went back to the bar.

"What?" asked Will.

I told him about the night Sam came to the house. When I got to the part where Sam grabbed and kissed me, Will jumped to his feet. "I'm going to have a talk with him," he said.

I grabbed Will's hand. "No. It was just a kiss, and I haven't seen him since."

"You bit him?"

"I thought it made the point better than words."

We finished our drinks. Sam stared at us as we went out the door.

CHAPTER 6

When the season changed and the air turned cool, there was finally a lull at the store. Haying was mostly done, and the farmers were busy chopping corn for silage. People had stopped buying seeds months ago, although ladies from town still came in for bulbs to plant in their flower gardens. Peggy and I were celebrating the easier days with some fresh coffee that we were sipping behind the counter. She suggested that I talk to Will about getting married.

"It's time to drop a hint about making things permanent," she said.

"What do you mean?"

Peggy crossed her legs and leaned back in her chair. "One man brought up marriage with me, and that was Fidelio." She paused and looked out the window. "Either you can wait around hoping somebody asks you, or you can do something about it."

I knew Will wanted marriage and kids, but I didn't know if he wanted those things with me. I liked Will. I felt safe with him. He'd told me his family owned the farm, so there was no mortgage. Will was an only child, and everything would go to him when his parents died. Will said the farm had one-hundred-ninety-seven acres, which meant he was land rich. I didn't know if he had any money though, to buy things like a wedding ring.

I invited him to the house for dinner.

We ate in the dining room. It was so tiny, it barely fit a table and four chairs. I set the table with Mama's good china, and made meatloaf and baked potatoes. Will ate without talking. When he was done, a trail of crumbs led from the bread dish to his plate, and he said, "Good." For desert, we ate apple pie I had baked the night before, and drank coffee from cups decorated in a pattern of violets and ivy.

"You like kids?" I asked.

"You need kids on a farm to help with chores."

"So you'd like to get married one day?" I took a sip of coffee and smiled.

"I thought about it."

I put my cup down and smiled some more. "Have you thought about us getting married?"

"Why are you smiling so much?"

"People who care for each other should get married. It's the way things are supposed to be."

"So do you care for me, or are you saying you want to get married?"

I looked down at my coffee cup. Why did I ever listen to Peggy?

Will leaned over and took my hand. "Why don't you come over and meet the folks then?" He winked at me.

After he left, I went upstairs to bed and snuggled under my quilt. I wondered what it would be like seeing Will every day for the rest of my life. I wondered what it would be like living on a farm. Will said it could get lonely, as there weren't any close neighbors. I knew about lonely. Mama, Daddy and I lived on the edge of town, and we could walk to the center in twenty minutes, but we rarely did, because somebody was always home sick. We saw Mrs. Baleen regularly, but that was about it. I shouldn't have a problem with more loneliness, as long as Will and Daddy were around to keep me company. Will said on a farm, no matter how hard you worked, things could still go wrong. There were things you just couldn't control, like a long spell of bad weather. I was used to illness, so I knew about things you couldn't control. I wondered if farm life would be too hard for me. I wondered if I was making a mistake. Then Will's face jumped into my head, and a sense of comfort washed over me. He would protect me. He would help me finish paying off the taxes. I would eventually be co-owner of one-hundred-ninety-seven acres of land. Mrs. Bishop would take notice. Daddy would be pleased.

The next Saturday night, Will came by to pick me up for supper at the farm.

"Anybody home?" Will shouted up the stairs.

I shouted back that I'd be down in a minute. He was drinking from a can of beer when I came into the kitchen. I always had a six-pack cooling for him in the fridge. His skin looked raw from shaving. A tiny piece of tissue paper stuck to his jaw with a drop of blood.

I did a pirouette in my blue dress. "How do I look?"

"Good." Will pressed me to him and kissed my mouth. I smelled the beer.

"I want to make a good impression on your folks."

We went out to the truck. Will opened the door and quickly dusted off the seat with his hand. He moved an axe, a sledgehammer, and a box of fencing nails to the back of the truck. "I was so late, I didn't have time to clean up inside the truck before I came over," he said.

He took a long look at my legs as I climbed in. As he drove, Will said how lucky he was, finding a blonde pixie with soft hands and dark eyes out here in the sticks. He had almost given up hope that he would ever find anyone, and then he went to the Co-Op and there I was. Will said it was good I was young and could learn to adjust to farm life. Maybe I'd help him in the barn a little, if kids didn't come along right away. If I just took it slow, I'd be okay.

I didn't think it would be hard at all, living on a dairy farm, so I barely listened. I was going to be the wife of a landowner, and that would make me an important person. I'd walk around the farmhouse in a frilly dress, prune roses in the summer, and cook roasts in the winter.

We drove past the grain bins at the train depot and took a left turn over the railroad tracks to Taylor Road. The first place we passed had freshly painted buildings, and the landscaping was so beautiful, it looked like the farm belonged in a magazine. Will said a retired stockbroker from New York City lived there. An elderly couple who boarded dogs owned the next place. A little further along, there was a farm that belonged to an old man and his son. Everything looked like it needed repair, from the barn door, to the fences, to the stones around a beautiful lilac bush in the flower bed near the house.

After a few miles of open fields, the road changed from tar to dirt. I had to brace myself as the truck bounded over bumps in the road. Rocks hit the undercarriage, making dull thuds. Will slowed the truck and turned onto a long, uphill driveway, where the shape of four buildings defined the horizon: a house, two barns, and a garage.

Will's dog Benny, a dark-haired collie, ran over and sniffed me as I got out of the truck. He poked my knee with his cool, wet nose, and followed me with his tail perked up like a flagpole as we went into the house. We entered a long hallway with a black floor, pegs on the wall for jackets, an area for boots, and a straight-back chair with a wicker seat. We went through another door into the kitchen. Benny squeezed past us and walked in a circle before lying down near his dish.

A woman stood at the stove, stirring something in a large pot. She wore loose jeans, sneakers, and a flannel shirt. She was tall, and somehow made the old clothes look elegant. Her face had wrinkles around the mouth. Her eyes were like Will's. He introduced her as his mother, Belle Phelps.

"Call me Belle," she said, as she took my hand.

Will introduced me to his father, Ed Phelps, who was standing by the table. While Belle was tall and thin, Ed was short and pleasantly overweight. He wore overalls and brown slippers. He clutched the end of a pipe between his teeth and held a newspaper in his hand.

"I can see why Will ain't been home much lately," said Ed. He winked at me. He said he had gone to school with my father. "I had to drop out in the eighth grade when my pa died."

"Same thing happened to me, although I was a little older," I said.

"Then we'll have lots of stories to swap," said Ed. He winked again.

Except for the electric lights and refrigerator, the kitchen might have looked this way a hundred years ago. Dominating the room was a cast iron stove with enamel sides that held nothing more than the memory of a shine. The walls were rough, and the beams in the ceiling were dark. The pine floorboards had deep marks from wear. Across from the fridge sat a set of cabinets, a long counter, and a sink. The room smelled of burning wood.

Belle moved the pot to the side of the stove. "Let's show you around while there's still some light outside."

We followed her into the hallway. Belle took a coat from a peg and put it on. "Ed don't like to put his shoes back on once he's in for the night, so it'll just be us."

Belle looked at my shoes, a pair of black pumps. "Put these on," she said, handing me a pair of boots. "I'd hate for you to ruin those."

We went across the driveway toward the barn. Belle said that she and Ed had bought the place from Mrs. Cook, who had included everything in the sale: furniture, farm equipment, hand tools, and even the pots and pans. Belle said Mrs. Cook's great grandparents chose the property for the ridge around the house, giving sweeping views of the land and surrounding hills. Belle gestured toward the pasture across the road. The green was dotted with juniper bushes that decorated the terrain as it rose and fell in a gigantic stationary wave.

"Will was born here. He came to us late in life. I didn't think I was ever going to get pregnant, and then all of a sudden, there he was. As soon as he could walk, he'd run off to the pasture. I couldn't go with him all the time, 'cause there's always so much to do on a farm. I kept an eye on him from the front windows, though. Then he started going into the barn with his father, and that's where he stayed. He took to farming like a bird takes to a breeze." Belle smiled at Will, and he smiled back.

We went into the milking parlor that Ed and Will had built. The room was cool and very clean. A large stainless-steel storage tank stood in the middle of the room, with a paddle inside to stir and cool the milk. Mounted on the far wall was a pump that provided suction for the milking machines.

We went through a door to a long building for the cows. Inside there were stanchions, a concrete floor, and siding on the walls.

The smell, a combination of ammonia and milk, hit me on my first breath. It reminded me of the scent of the fertilizer in the Co-Op, but this was much worse. I was going to smell that scent every time I went into the barn. I was marrying that smell. I started to sway. Will grabbed my arm.

"You haven't eaten all day, have you?" he asked.

"I had a bite at lunch." Why was Will asking me about food?

"Mom, let's finish up and get some food into Lily before she faints on us."

As we turned to leave, Will explained that he and Ed brought the milking machines to each cow individually. The milk went through a pipe hanging over the cows, directly into the tank. When they finished milking a cow, they removed the milking machine, and moved to another animal. They're milked twice a day, as Will put it, "In rain, snow, and even when I don't goddamn well feel like it."

"The siding on the walls is plastic, so we can scrub it to get the manure off," said Belle.

I imagined the brown splatter covering the walls, my hands, and my beautiful blue dress. Bile rose in my throat. I swallowed it down.

We went back outside, and peeked through dusty windows into the old barn next door. The modernized milking barn was smaller and very clean in comparison. Here, the stalls were dirty and the feeding troughs empty. A heavy coating of chaff covered everything, from the rafters down to the wooden floor. An immense cobweb decorated one window, with a spider the size of a ping-pong ball clinging to it. I stifled a scream.

"Cows don't go into the old barn anymore," said Belle. "We just keep calves in there now down at the other end, and store hay up in the rafters. We do all the milking and feeding in the new barn. Years ago, we used to milk in the old barn. The cows stood on the wooden floor over a huge cellar. I had to scrape the manure away with a hoe, open the trough, and let it fall onto the ground below. When enough built up, Ed would fill the spreader, and put it on the fields. He used to say you couldn't buy a better fertilizer."

I shuddered at the thought of manure falling through the air, and swayed again.

Will grabbed me by the waist. "That's the end of the tour, Mom. We're goin' in to eat."

We went back into the house. As I handed my coat to Will, I noticed Belle looking at me again. I shivered, partially from Belle's stare, and partially from the cold. Without a word, Belle went to a laundry basket on the far edge of the counter and pulled out a blue cardigan covered with lint balls. She draped it over my shoulders. I said thanks and wiggled into the warmth. It stretched all the way down to my knees. I had always been the one to guess other people's needs, whether it was a warm blanket for Daddy, or a cold compress for Mama. Belle's simple gesture meant that someone else was thinking about me for a change, and it made me feel welcome.

I sat in a chair next to Will and looked through an archway into a living and dining room. The wallpaper was a blast of red roses. A large table surrounded by chairs with red tapestry on the seats stood in the center of the room. A bookcase with ornate carving adorned the far wall, next to a fancy red velvet sofa that had no business being in a farmhouse.

Belle put the pots down on the table, on blocks of wood that protected the plastic. We ate stew and crusty brown bread. Between bites, Will mentioned that we were talking about getting married. Belle said the best time of the year was in the fall, after the corn crop was in.

"It's cool, and the grass is still green. Most of all, there's less work to do, 'cause the cows can still eat from the fields. We don't have to stay home to feed them during the day," said Belle. "How many people are you going to invite?"

I said, "Uh."

"I would think about fifty in all," said Belle.

"Let's have it at the Moose Lake Rod and Gun Club," said Ed. "They have a nice big room, and they got a bar." He turned to me. "You know where it is, don't ya?"

"Uh."

"We'll have a buffet," said Belle. "We'll kill a few turkeys. There's one the size of a small calf out in the pen. The neighbors will bring food. People always want to bring something. We'll have to get a cake. They could do it at the bakery in Willow Springs, but I don't know how much they charge. Maybe Annie Shipman would make one for us. Her cakes are so good they could cure the common cold. Do you have a dress?"

I thought of Mama's wedding dress in the chest at the foot of her bed and nodded.

"Perfect." Belle sat back in her chair. "You know, I think we got us a wedding." She smiled, looked at Will, and nodded. "All you kids gotta do is show up."

Will winked at me.

Ed stood, went to the cabinet, and came back with a bottle of whiskey and shot glasses. "We got something to celebrate, so let's celebrate." He filled each glass to the brim.

Belle held up her glass and said, "To love and marriage."

Ed said, "To the prettiest daughter-in-law in Willow Springs."

They drank their whiskey in one gulp, and I took a sip. As they continued to chat about the wedding, I sat back, the remains of the meal on the plate in front of me. I wasn't sure how events had gone so far and with such speed, but I didn't mind. I was part of a family again. As I listened to the banter, I realized that all I had to do was go along.

Later that night, I sat on the front steps in Mama's robe, with a cigarette between my fingers. I didn't cough any more from the smoke. I told Daddy that Will and I had picked a date. In a sudden revelation, I realized that Will had never actually proposed to me. However, we had a date, knew where the reception was going to be held, and who in general terms, we would invite. That son of a gun.

"I can see Grandpa Will fooling you into marrying him," said Angie. "He would have thought it was funny."

"He did."

"Did you love him when you got married?"

"I don't think an eighteen-year-old girl knows what love is," I said.

"Of course they do," said Angie.

"I stand corrected."

"With your daddy, it naturally went from thinking about him, to seeing him, didn't it Grandma?" Angie asked.

"It did. I think Daddy was worried about me. I was all alone, in debt, and that's why he came back."

"Ma worries about money all the time. Last September, Ma said she would give me twenty dollars so I could buy a few things for school, but she didn't have the money just then. Red took out his wallet and put twenty dollars on the table real slow, so she was sure to notice. She kissed him. Then when she turned away, he put the money back into his wallet."

"What did Claire say about that?"

"I didn't tell her. I figured she already had enough to worry about."

CHAPTER 7

One evening before the wedding, Will and I were in Belle's kitchen, eating a supper of roast pork, green beans, and baked potatoes. As Ed reached for the plate of bread, he said that he and Belle were going to retire and sign over the farm to Will and me as a wedding present.

"Now you really got to marry him," said Ed. He winked at me.

I expected us to own the farm eventually, but never so soon. I was surprised and humbled by the generosity of the gift. I was about to transform from a scared teenager into a woman of substance, like Mrs. Bishop who lived in a magnificent house and gave parties that I had only heard about. I would own acres of land and a farm. I sat up straighter in my chair. I had accomplished something. I couldn't wait to tell Daddy.

Will said, "Don't look so surprised. We were going to get it anyway, sooner or later."

Belle and Ed wanted a smaller house with a downstairs bedroom, so I sold them my house for enough money to cover the back taxes. It was a relief to be out of debt. The house was perfect for them, and not far away. It needed work, but Ed was looking forward to the challenge. I thought I got the better end of the deal. I didn't tell them about the ghosts.

A week before the wedding, I quit my job at the Co-Op, and promised Peggy I'd keep in touch. I brought a few things over to the farm: two suitcases, three boxes, and a 'Home Sweet Home' sampler that I had embroidered when I was ten years old. Mama had taught me how to embroider. She had also taught me enough about cooking so I could get by.

I stacked everything in the back hall.

The wedding was on the third Saturday in October. The corn crop was in and the haying was done.

That morning, I turned off the alarm before it rang, made coffee, and sipped it as I walked through the house. It was my last day living here. In a few hours, I would be Mrs. Will Phelps. I went into the room where Mama and Daddy had died, sat down on the bed, and lit a cigarette.

Daddy appeared, sitting in the chair next to the bed. He crossed his legs. I asked him if he wanted a cigarette. He said no.

I told Daddy that he had to stay out of sight when Will was around. Daddy nodded. Will might shoot Daddy dead again if he ever saw him. I figured that dying once in any lifetime was enough.

Then in a moment of panic, I said, "Daddy, how are you going to get to the farm? I'll never see you again! What am I going to do?"

"Don't worry Pumpkin. I'll find you."

I took a deep drag. "How did you know you really loved Mama?"

"You just know. You feel it."

I hadn't slept with Will yet, and he would expect to have sex tonight. I didn't want to do it, but maybe I would feel different after the ceremony. Maybe saying the words 'I do' would make me want sex. At least I hoped it would. I was nervous and queasy. I could call Will and say I had changed my mind, that I loved him, but I just couldn't go through with it. Then what would happen? Would I ever find anyone else? I would spend my life alone, get sick, and die.

Someone knocked at the door. It was Peggy, to help me get ready. She had on a blue dress and a hat with white feathers.

We went into the back bedroom, where Mama's wedding dress hung down from the light fixture in the middle of the ceiling. The train went all the way to the floor, making the dress look like it belonged to a very tall woman. The dress moved when we opened the door, and I saw Mama peeking out from behind it. It was nice that she came by on my wedding day.

Peggy grabbed a chair, climbed up, got the dress down, and plopped it onto the bed. I don't think she saw Mama.

"Mothers are supposed to talk to their daughters on their wedding day," said Peggy as she arranged my hair. "Your mama's dead, so I'm gonna tell you a few things that I had to learn for myself."

I held my breath.

"When you're a couple, you need to put out when he wants it, or else he'll find it somewhere else," said Peggy.

"Will's not like that."

"There's nothin' wrong with Will. I ain't saying there's something wrong with him. But he's a man, ain't he?"

I half-listened to Peggy's ramblings, nodding occasionally. I swooned at the soft touch of the makeup brush, and Peggy's cool fingers on my back as she buttoned Mama's dress.

Finally, Peggy looked at the clock and said, "We better get moving, or you're gonna miss your own wedding."

I stared at myself in the mirror, entranced by the reflection of a familiar stranger whose future was about to change. The dress had faded to the delicate color of old paper. The veil hung down over my shoulders from a barrette covered in silk flowers. My skin glowed with porcelain perfection. I was beautiful, and yet, with yellow hair and red lips, I was the cheap plastic bride that belonged on top of a wedding cake.

Peggy poked me in the side. "We gotta go."

I thought of Daddy as I went toward the car. Would he be at the ceremony? How would he get there? I got in the backseat of the old Chevy, and Peggy folded the train over my lap so it wouldn't wrinkle.

We drove fast over the dirt road toward the Moose Lake Rod and Gun Club. The second time my head hit the roof, I said, "Slow down, or I'm gonna throw up."

"I don't want to be late."

As we continued to bounce down the road, I thought back to the previous afternoon, when Will and I had gone to the Rod and Gun Club to see how Belle and her friends had decorated the place. It was a simple, one-story building, nestled in the woods next to the lake. The large room inside had a bar at one end, rest rooms at the other end, and a wall of windows overlooking the water. Tables and chairs were set up all over the room. There was a long table under the windows for the buffet. Each table had a white paper tablecloth, and a small vase with marigolds and asters. A paper chandelier hung from the ceiling, with white streamers stretched to the corners of the room.

A trellis with a paper heart hanging down from the center marked the corner where the ceremony would take place. Will stood under the paper heart to see if it hit his head. It did, and we both laughed like nervous teenagers.

As we walked around the room, Will said that Belle had roasted three turkeys, and one was so big, she had to cut it in half with a butcher knife to get it into the oven. Belle said that people were going to bring vegetable dishes, homemade bread, relishes, sodas for the kids, and enough beer to give everyone a good time.

Will said, "Marriage is going to be good for us, you'll see."

"Sounds like you're trying to talk yourself into it."

"I'm sure. How about you?"

I popped out of my daydream when Peggy screeched to a halt in front of the Rod and Gun Club. "You ready?"

I felt queasy.

Peggy helped me out of the car. I told her I didn't want to go inside just yet.

"Why on earth wouldn't you want to go inside?" Peggy put her hands on her hips.

"I want to make an entrance."

"I'll wait out here with you, then."

"I want to be alone for a few minutes."

"You always want to be alone. What're you getting married for?"

"It's my day, and you have to do what I say." I kissed Peggy on the cheek, and she went inside. I swept the train of my dress over my arm and walked down the gravel path to the picnic tables by the water. Moose Lake glimmered so brightly, it was as though the sun was shining up from under the surface. I saw Will's eyes where the dark blue faded to green.

I thought about Mama's wedding. I wondered if she had been happy, or nervous and unsure of herself, like me.

Mama's sickness had defined my youth. Daddy took care of things during the day when I was at school. When I got home at three o'clock, he left for work at the mill. I made supper and fed Mama. She only ate soup and mashed-up vegetables. I read the paper to her. Then I rubbed her back and legs with isopropyl alcohol. Her skin was so papery, I thought it might tear.

I had to coax Mama to take her pills.

"Those things are nothin' but poison. You trying to poison me?" she asked.

Usually, she spat the pills out into her hand and left them there, melting into her skin. I took them from her hand and put them on the nightstand next to the clock with the big face. The pills left white stains on the tablecloth. They were always there in the morning, so I picked them up and flushed them down the toilet.

After dark, I sat in a chair by the bed and waited for the ranting to begin.

"Are the taxes paid?" Mama sat up in the bed and looked at me with fearful eyes.

"I don't know, Mama."

One night, she asked, "Who are you?"

I looked down at Mama's dress billowing around me in the breeze, and wondered if I was going to become crazy from a sickness that ate my brain. I wondered if Will and the kids we might have would care for me like I had cared for Mama and Daddy.

I walked back to the Rod and Gun, and listened for the music that was my cue to enter. Peggy had told me the name of the song, but I forgot what it was. If I entered when they were playing the wrong song, everybody would think I was an idiot. I finally heard music. It had to be the right song. If I went inside, it would be the right song, even if it wasn't.

I stood up straight, took a breath, and prepared to become a bride.

I turned the doorknob and pushed. A gust of wind suddenly picked up, fluffed out my dress, and pushed my veil forward. It was as if nature was telling me to get on with it. The doorknob flew out of my hand, and the door slammed against the wall. Everybody looked at me, with my dress swaying around my legs as if it belonged to a dancing ghost. Leaves flew into the room. The paper chandelier rocked back and forth. The vases on the tables fell over, and the edges of the tablecloths flew into the air. Hands reached out to smooth the crinkling paper and upright the vases. Everyone stood. A little boy raced toward me, making squeaking noises. I wanted to hold his hand so I wouldn't have to walk alone. His mother waddled up, grabbed him by the arm, and led him back to a table.

As I walked toward Will, I was nervous and felt out of place, amid a sea of cotton print dresses and mothball suits.

The minister wore a high school graduation robe. As he talked about what marriage meant, I watched Will's hands. They were oversized, and the skin was dark from the sun. The knuckles were rough and scarred. Creases in the skin looked as though a child had traced over them with a black marker. The closest thing the nails had ever come to a manicure was the blade of a pocketknife. My eyes rose to his chest and the yellow aster in his lapel. I looked at his mouth curved up in a smile, and then his eyes that glimmered like the lake outside.

"Yes," I blurted out.

Everyone laughed. My face got hot. I was an idiot.

The minister turned to me and asked, "Do you take this man, Will Phelps, to be your lawfully wedded husband?"

I said yes again.

After the ceremony, the crowd clapped, and came up to congratulate us. When Mrs. Baleen hugged me, she picked me up off the floor.

The teenagers played records, and everyone ate. The party broke up around four o'clock, when it was time to go home and milk the cows. Will and I left for three nights in a motel outside of Sturbridge. Belle knew the owners, so they'd given us a good price that included breakfast.

The motel had a steep front lawn, and parking in the back. Will carried our suitcases up the stairs, unlocked the door, and flopped down on the bed. The room had a little refrigerator.

"Come here," he said.

It was the moment I dreaded. "I'm hungry."

"We just ate."

I shrugged. Will looked at me, sighed, and got up off the bed.

We ate turkey and gravy at a diner about a mile down the road. I stretched the meal out for as long as I could. I didn't want sex, plain and simple. The ceremony hadn't made me want sex, as I had hoped it would. I wished I had thought more about this part of married life before saying, "I do." Now sex was going to be part of my job as a wife. I really liked Will. He made me feel safe. Maybe it wouldn't be so bad. Maybe it would be better just to get it over with.

"Let's go back to the motel," I said.

Will paid the check quicker than a hungry kid could gobble a piece of candy.

When we got to the room, Will said, "Let's go to bed."

I went into the bathroom and put on the nightgown Peggy had given me. It was short, black, and had a little bow woven through the lace around the neck.

I got into bed. Will was already under the sheets, and he didn't have any clothes on. He kissed me. He smelled of fresh hay and bar soap. As he ran his hands over my back, the image of a man with a swollen nose and crooked lips came to me in a flash of pain that started in my head and went down to my toes. It was the face from my nightmares. The face had made me scream when I was a little girl. I wanted to scream now.

I pushed Will away.

"What's the matter?" he asked.

I couldn't tell him about the face from my nightmare, just as I couldn't tell him that I smoked to conjure up my Daddy, or that I got fearful every time I went into my kitchen at home. I couldn't let Will regret marrying me already. I had to give us a chance to be happy. I had to keep my secrets tucked away. I had to calm down.

I pulled him back to me. I had to try.

Will rubbed my back, and I shivered in fear of what was to come. I closed my eyes and tried to think of something else.

"You like it when I rub your back, huh?" asked Will.

As his tongue traced circles on my neck, he squeezed me in a way that made my insides recoil.

When I opened my eyes, Will's hair had turned white, his lips had become crooked, and his nose had swollen. The face from my nightmare was on Will's body. Before I could gasp, the lips covered mine. Then a voice that wasn't Will's told me what to do, what to touch, what to stroke. The words jumbled my brain. The words became marbles bouncing in my head, clacking against the inside of my skull. I couldn't think. I couldn't react. There was only the shock of the marbles hitting the inside of my head, and the voice that wasn't Will's saying my name.

I had to obey. I was a good girl.

I moved my hand below Will's belly. I did what the voice told me to do, as my head throbbed in pain.

Will moaned.

Maybe it would be quick, like pulling a tooth, like pricking a finger, and then Will's face would be back. He lowered his weight on me.

I closed my eyes, and prayed to be somewhere else. Suddenly, I was. I was a speck of dust floating over the bed. I saw Will's back. I saw my knees and my face. I looked scared. I floated out the window, over the motel and the cars in the parking lot. I was a butterfly, a bird, a creature of the wind. I was free. I soared over the tops of the trees. I floated on my back with my hands crossed under my head and looked up at the stars. I wondered if there really was a heaven. I wondered where Daddy went when he wasn't with me. I flipped over and moved my arms and legs as if I was swimming. I drifted across the road to the valley, where even the trees looked purple in the dark. A violet mist hung over the grass. Daddy joined me as I floated over the purple trees, and we talked until Will was done.

Afterward, when Will and I were lying together, with my head resting on his shoulder, he said, "I loved it when you touched me there. It was so exciting. Where did you learn to do that?"

"I shouldn't be hearing this," said Angie.

"You need to hear the whole story. Claire doesn't know how it was between Will and me, not really."

"Sex is supposed to be fun."

"Sex can be complicated."

"But I'm an impressionable teenager."

"Sometimes you're a pain in my backside."

Angie made a face.

"I often thought I'd be a happy woman, if only we stopped having sex. Will took care of me, and I did what I had to do, to make him happy. Besides, it was good having someone to talk to besides Daddy." I took a sip of coffee. "This is cold. I'll make a fresh pot."

I went into the kitchen and stood at the window over the sink, staring off into the trees. I brushed a tear from my cheek. I turned. Angie was standing next to me.

"Let me help," she said.

When the coffee was ready, Angie put it on a tray and carried it into the living room. We sat down, and she poured some into cups. "You miss him, don't you?"

"Every second."

"I bet the farm looked different back then."

"And your house, too. Ed made a lot of changes when he and Belle lived there, before you and your mother moved in. I think I have some photographs from when I was a girl. Want to see?"

I went to the bedroom and opened the door to the closet. I held one of Will's shirts to my face and breathed in his scent: fresh hay and bar soap. For a second, it was as if Will was with me again.

I pulled down the album from the shelf and brought it to Angie. I opened it over her lap and guided her through the pictures, one by one, remembering how bright Mama's eyes were before she got sick, and how handsome Daddy was. I touched the picture of Will standing in front of the barn on our wedding day, all dressed up, with a yellow aster in his lapel, and Benny sitting next to him. I was pleased that Angie seemed genuinely interested.

When we finished looking at the pictures, I went on with my story.

CHAPTER 8

The morning after we got back from Sturbridge, I went down the farmhouse stairs, pausing at each step to look at the blossoming apple trees on the wallpaper around me. I was a queen, but in exchange for my castle, I had to watch my husband transform into the monster from my nightmares. I didn't know how long I could stand it. Peggy went through men as fast as a hot knife through butter, but she liked sex. Maybe she was lucky after all.

I thought Will might surprise me and have breakfast waiting, but no one was in the kitchen. I heard the hum of the milking machine. Will was in the barn. I brewed coffee in the electric pot, poured myself a cup, sat down at the table, and examined my domain.

The soot from the stove exaggerated the roughness of the hand-plastered walls. The refrigerator was the color of parchment. The antique wood stove was covered in grime and rust. The wood box, marred by dings and dents, was the same green color as the window trim. Circles of dirt surrounded the cabinet pulls, making them look like black eyes. The floor was dark in the corners, and covered with scratches. It needed to be sanded and varnished, or better yet, covered with linoleum, maybe black and white squares. I was overwhelmed. I sat with my hands on my lap and let my coffee get cold.

Will came in around nine o'clock. He crossed the room and kissed me. Benny sniffed my knees and then curled up next to the stove.

I asked Will what he wanted for breakfast.

"I usually have half a dozen eggs. Scrambled. Toast and butter," he said.

I pointed at the cast iron cook stove. "On that?"

Will nodded. Belle cooked on the wood stove, but it never occurred to me that I would actually be using it. Besides, it was my first morning on the farm. I didn't want to handle wood to start a fire, let alone do the cooking. But I didn't want to start my marriage by complaining, so I put paper and a nice big piece of wood into the firebox and lit a match. After the paper burned up, the fire went out.

"Let me show you what to do," said Will.

He took out the piece of wood and set it aside. Then he put paper and kindling into the firebox. He adjusted the dampers and lit the paper with a match. When the kindling was crackling, he added a few small pieces of wood. When that was burning, he added a few larger pieces. Then he readjusted the dampers.

"It's going to take a while for the stove to get hot, so I may as well go do something, or else nothin'll get done," said Will. He left the room with Benny at his heels.

I watched them through the window. Will was limping. His foot must hurt, and that meant it was going to rain. Will had told me that he had gone into the woods with the chainsaw some years ago. The saw bucked when it hit a knot in the log he was cutting. His mind was on something else, and he didn't have a good grip on the saw. The blade went into his foot. There was a lot of blood in the truck by the time he got home. Belle applied a tourniquet, and Ed drove like a maniac to the clinic, with his feet in his son's blood covering the floor of the truck.

Will told me that the nurse had said "Ugh," when she saw his foot. She said he might have died if it wasn't for the tourniquet.

I took three aspirins out of a jar on the counter and put them next to Will's coffee cup. Then I put a pan on the stove and added a spoonful of butter. It stared at me like a yellow eye. Will came in later and washed his hands at the sink. The toast had just popped out of the toaster, and the eggs were ready.

After breakfast, we decided to go to town for groceries.

"Let's stop at Cooper's," I said. "Maybe we can look at the electric stoves." I didn't want to use that dirty wood-burning stove again.

"I got to buy a mower this year. A few second-hand ones should come up soon, and I got to have the cash ready if I want to get one cheap. I'll get you a new stove when we can afford it."

"I want to paint the kitchen, too."

"I'll do it for you honey, but I got to finish chopping wood for winter, and the tractor needs a new clutch. Then I got to fix the tire on the trailer."

We parked in front of Cooper's Hardware, and went inside. The room was dark, except for the area near the windows, where Mr. Cooper sat reading a newspaper. He was wearing baggy pants, a brown sweater, a white shirt, and a bowtie. The air smelled dusty.

"Hi there, Will. Is this the new missus?"

"Lily, you know Mr. Cooper," said Will.

Mr. Cooper stretched out his hand. The skin around the knuckles sagged. I took it and quickly let go.

"Let me turn the lights on for ya," said Mr. Cooper. He shuffled to a bank of switches on the wall. Each made a dull clacking sound as he moved it to the 'on' position. The room expanded as the lights shone down from the ceiling.

I moved down the center aisle to the paint supplies, between shelves loaded with nuts, bolts, and power tools. I picked out two gallons of white gloss, a brush, a roller, and a paint tray, and handed them to Will. I went over the creaking floor to Mr. Cooper, who was standing behind the cash register.

"Gonna be paintin' there, Will?" asked Mr. Cooper.

Will shrugged, paid the bill, and we left to get the groceries.

The next morning, I put on an old pair of jeans, one of Will's work shirts, and sneakers. I went down to the kitchen, stood in the center of the room, and looked at the dull walls. I was glad I knew how to paint. After all, I had painted my old kitchen.

By lunchtime, I had finished two walls. Will came in, hooked his cap on the back of his chair, and sat down.

"What's that smell?" he asked.

"Belle left some stew for us."

"It ain't that."

"It must be the paint."

"Lil, you're working for nothing. That stove puts out a lot of soot and the walls are going to look like hell in no time."

"I think it looks better." I was a little annoyed that Will didn't appreciate my efforts to improve the place.

"I don't want you to be disappointed."

I bit my lip, dished out the stew, and asked him what he was doing outside.

"I have a pile of wood that needs to be split into pieces that can fit into the stove. Then I need to toss it into the woodshed, so it'll stay dry. Dad's coming over this afternoon to give me a hand. Don't worry. I ain't gonna let you freeze this winter." Will glanced at the walls, ate his lunch, and then left when Ed's truck pulled into the driveway.

Later, Ed came into the house. I was painting the wall behind the stove.

"Did you scrub those walls before painting?" asked Ed.

"No, why?"

"They're covered with grease and soot. If you don't scrub 'em down first, the paint won't stick, no matter what you do. If you're gonna do the job, you may as well do it right."

Ed must have seen the look of disappointment on my face. "Don't worry. I'll help you fix it."

Every morning for the rest of the week, Ed and I sanded, scrubbed, primed, and repainted the walls. We started working early, when Will was milking in the barn, and stopped just before he came in for lunch.

We ate a lot of sandwiches that week.

Finally, Will said, "Lil, the walls look better every time I see them. I guess I never noticed how bad they really were."

When Ed and I finished painting, the walls were perfect. But by spring, they were gray and dull again, from the soot given off by the wood stove.

One day, I had every single window open downstairs, trying to get the breeze to push out the scent of the pork roast I had made for lunch. Will was working in the garage, and the leftover roast was still on the table. I stood at the kitchen window and lit a cigarette. I took a few long drags, thought of Daddy, and before I knew it, he was standing right next to me. I was so happy to see him. I showed him around, and he said it was a big place. We sat at the table, chatting and smoking. I heard a noise at the door, and my stomach went into my throat. I thought it was Will taking off his boots. He didn't know I smoked. I jumped up and ran to put the ashtray on the shelf over the stove. I fanned the air and told Daddy he'd better disappear, or he'd have a lot of explaining to do.

I waited, but the door didn't open. A minute later, there was another noise. I got up to open the door, and in came Benny. He brushed past me, went to his empty dish, and sniffed it. I got the ashtray, lit another cigarette, and sat down. Daddy was back by then, and I said, "False alarm."

Benny came over to me, sat on his hind legs, and looked at the table where the roast was cooling. He barked once, high and quick. I told Benny it was just Daddy. Benny whimpered and looked at his dish. Daddy was a stranger to Benny, so I put one hand on the back of Daddy's chair, and the other hand on Benny's head. He lifted his snout and sniffed the air, which now smelled of pork roast and cigarette smoke.

"Daddy, pat Benny's head."

"I don't like dogs."

I told Benny to go lie down. He stopped at his dish, looked at me, and then stretched out in front of the stove.

I got into a routine. When I got up in the morning, I did all the cooking for the day. I made breakfast for Will and something for dinner. I made stews, roast chicken, and soups from leftovers. It was just Will and me, but he ate enough for three people, so I made sure I cooked plenty. I put the food on the side of the stove, where it would stay warm until Will came inside to eat. That gave me a stretch of time to do whatever I wanted.

After painting the kitchen, Ed showed me how to sand and stain the cabinet doors. They were dark when we started, but after cleaning off the grime, the wood was light. I chose a honey-colored stain and was very happy with the results. Unfortunately, they made the rest of the room look even worse.

Around milking time, I went into the barn and watched Will work. I sat on a bin that Ed had made to hold sawdust. It was near the door, which I kept open so the barn smell wouldn't bother me so much. I dangled my feet over the side of the bin. Benny sat on the floor next to me.

Will talked to every single cow. I was surprised he knew them so well, because they were just cows, but he was with them every day, so it made sense.

"Time for your mastitis treatment, Mildred."

"How about some balm for that rash, Cupcake?"

He felt a cow's underbelly and said, "You're going to be having your calf today, aren't you girl?"

"Don't let me forget to order grain tomorrow, Bessie."

"Will, do you expect that cow to tell you to order the grain?" I asked.

"Wouldn't it be something if she did?"

"I could remind you."

"That'd be nice, Lil. Thanks."

Will never rushed when he was working in the barn. If a cow wanted to stand for a while before going out the door, he'd let her. They'd look at the barnyard together. He'd talk about the weather or local politics, and she'd respond by snorting or swishing her tail. When she finally moved, Will went back to his chores.

After the milking was done, and the cows were outside for the night, Will grabbed a hoe and scraped manure into the trough. When he got to the end of the barn, he turned on the switch to the barn cleaner. Its metal arms pushed the waste outside, through a hole in the wall and onto a pile. He'd come over to me and fill a basket with sawdust from the bin, and toss some on the floor so the cows wouldn't slip. Eventually, he called out to me instead of Bessie, telling me to remind him to order supplies, or call Ken Shipman to come over for a cow, or a hundred other things. He said I should think about doing a few chores, like taking care of the calves in the spring, after I had adjusted to the life.

Then he went into the milking parlor and checked that the electricity was off. He washed off his boots with water from a hose and went toward the house, with Benny and me walking beside him.

Will told me he had found Benny at the old sawmill that was on the farm. Mrs. Cook's son had bought it, before taking up drinking as an occupation. The sawmill had a frame with a track, a carriage for the logs, and a diesel engine. As the logs passed by a circular saw, it cut the wood into planks.

Will was there to see what condition things were in, as he hadn't been in the woods since he had cut his foot with the chainsaw. He saw a dog watching him from a distance. After a while, it came up to him. The dog was scrawny and shivering. There was no collar. Will wanted to take him home and call a few neighbors to see if he belonged to anyone. The animal was too weak to jump onto the back of the truck, so Will lifted him up. Belle came outside when they drove up to the house.

"I think he's starving," said Will.

"Then let's feed him," said Belle.

Belle put some leftover ground beef, bread, and warm milk into a bowl. The collie ate the food, licked Will's hand, and fell asleep on the back of the truck.

No one knew whose dog it was. Will said that somebody probably drove out to the country and let the dog go. People did that sometimes, when they wanted to get rid of their pets. Will said it was a terrible thing to do. Dogs were valuable, and so were cats, to keep the mouse population down. Most dogs could be trained to bark at strangers. A smart one would herd cows. The ones who weren't so smart would at least keep you company.

From the day he gulped down Belle's concoction of beef and bread, Benny stayed home, unless Will went somewhere. Whenever Will got into the pickup truck, Benny jumped onto the back. They drove off together, Benny with his mouth open and his tongue flapping in the wind. Eventually, Benny followed me too, especially on walks in the pasture. But in the mornings and afternoons, Benny always sat next to the sawdust bin in the barn, while Will milked the cows.

One evening, the sunset was unusually beautiful as Benny, Will and I went back to the house.

"Let's go for a walk before supper," I said.

"But we haven't eaten yet."

"It's so nice out. Let's go down to the stream."

"What for?"

"We can walk along the road then."

"My foot hurts."

"We can watch the sunset together."

"I'm awful tired, Lil. I just want to go in the house and sit down."

Sometimes over supper, Will rambled on about the farm. When we first got married, money was tight, as Will was saving every penny for a badly-needed mower. He said if a machine broke down or production slacked off, he'd have to find another way to make a few bucks. Maybe he'd buy a few calves from Ken Shipman, raise them, and sell them for beef in a year or two. Will said that beef cattle in the field were as good as money in the bank.

"Why don't you give up the cows and just raise cattle?" I asked.

"In the long run, you make more money with dairy, and the price of milk is steady. The price of beef goes up and down, so you need a lot more animals and the land to feed them. We got a lot of woods on the farm, so we have to keep the size of the herd down. Besides, dairy is what I know best."

"I could go back to work at the Co-Op."

Will looked at me for a second, as if he was making up his mind. "When my parents lived here, the three of us put in fourteen-hour days, and we didn't get everything done. Of course, the herd was bigger then. I cut it down after Dad retired, so I could handle things by myself. You're taking care of the house, and I'd rather have you home, picking up chores little by little. The money will work itself out. Besides, if I have my way, you'll have a baby to take care of before too long."

"You didn't ask me if I wanted to go back to work."

"Do you?"

"Not really, but if I wanted to, you'd let me, wouldn't you?"

"Sure, Lil."

After supper most nights, Will read to me from the paper while I did the dishes. Then we watched TV, and Will nodded off in his chair.

The nap gave him energy for sex. It still bothered me something terrible, but soon I could float out the window as easy as snapping my fingers.

Sometimes I wondered about getting pregnant. Would I be a good mother? Did I want children? Daddy said I should have a family, but Will was my family. He wanted kids. As soon as Will started kissing me, I floated out the window, so I didn't think I was ever going to get pregnant.

Angie stared into the fire. "Grandpa Will always cared about you. He never said anything bad about you, even when you weren't around."

"He never talked about people behind their backs."

"Red was nice to me when Ma was around, but when she wasn't, he'd tell me that I was ugly and to lose weight so I'd look like something. First time he said it, he laughed, like he was making a joke, but it wasn't funny to me. I've asked him to stop calling me Fat Girl, but he just ignores me. I'm not fat, am I Grandma?"

"They're just words, Angie." I hoped that words were all there was between Red and my granddaughter.

"It still hurts."

"I think you're beautiful."

CHAPTER 9

One night during the winter, I looked out the front window and noticed how dark it was outside. Daddy could have been dancing a jig on the driveway and I wouldn't have seen it. The pasture across the road could have been anything: an ocean, a mountain, or a cathedral with spires that reached up to the stars. It was just too dark to tell.

We were going to Ken and Annie Shipman's house for supper. I switched on the porch light and walked carefully across the driveway, holding a warm apple pie in my hands. Annie was a fine cook, and I wanted to impress her with my ability in the kitchen. I had spent all afternoon making the pie. It looked perfect, and I couldn't wait for Annie to taste it. I smelled Will's aftershave as he ran past me to the truck.

The engine was running by the time I climbed into the passenger seat.

Eventually, we took a sharp turn to the left. The headlights bounced up and down as we went over ruts in the long driveway leading to the Shipman house. It was a relief when Will stopped the truck. I followed him as we walked in without knocking. Although I knew Ken from when he used to visit Daddy, and Annie had made my wedding cake, this was the first time I had been inside their home.

"There you are," said Annie. Her curls bounced as she talked. She cradled a stack of plates on her arm. "Will, why don't you grab a few beers, and go visit Ken until supper's ready? He's out in his office."

I put the pie on the side of the stove, and Annie said I shouldn't have brought anything. Will opened the fridge, grabbed the beers, and left, holding the necks of two bottles.

"Ken fixed up the old grain shed to use as an office. There isn't enough room to run a business in this relic of a house." Annie took my coat. "When he moved a TV out there, I knew I'd be spending a lot more time alone."

"How does he stay warm?"

"He has a space heater, and after a few beers, the cold really doesn't bother him."

I moved to the stove and rubbed my hands together.

"You look chilled. I'll make us a drink. My grandmother used to make it when I had a cold. I guess I just kept drinking it when I grew up."

Annie poured hot water into a mug and then added honey, a teabag, lemon, and some whiskey. I sipped the sweet mixture as I looked around the room. The wood stove shone like a new copper penny. Mine was as dull as cow dung. Next to it stood a white electric stove, covered with pots. It was the kind of stove I needed in my own kitchen. The sink and fridge were near the door. A large table with six chairs and cushions on the seats dominated the middle of the room.

After setting the table, Annie took me on a tour of the downstairs. We went along a back hallway to the dining and living rooms on the other side of the house. The walls had wood paneling on the bottom and wallpaper on the top. Annie called it wainscoting. The wide floorboards moaned as we walked over them. Every item was old, but clean and polished. It was how a country house should look. When Annie turned the light on to show me the antique banister in the front foyer, I gasped. Wallpaper with dancing spoons surrounded me: caramel candy spoons on a background of sunshine yellow. It was the same wallpaper that had hung in my kitchen.

My head started to spin. The spoons swirled around me. I was back in the old house. Mama was in the hospital and Daddy was visiting her. The man with the crooked lips and swollen nose from my nightmares was in the kitchen with me. Something hard was pressed against my throat, and he was talking. I couldn't hear what he was saying, because Annie was talking, too.

"Are you okay?"

"We had that wallpaper in the kitchen when I was a girl," I said, shivering.

"You must like it then."

"I hate it."

"Oh?"

"Can I use your bathroom?"

I ran water in the sink and sat on the edge of the tub. I wanted to go back to the farm and curl up in bed. Daddy had said it was a good thing Mama didn't die at home, because I would have been alone in the house with a dead mother. We had spent the whole day sitting at her bedside in the hospital, saying nothing, stretching out our time with her. Daddy brought me home around four o'clock in the afternoon. He told me to have a sandwich and try to get some rest. Then he went back to the hospital. I lay on the bed in Mama's room and watched the clock on the nightstand. I counted the seconds as the hands moved around the face of the clock. Little bits of time filled the room as I waited for Daddy to come home, and tell me whether Mama was alive or dead. It was as though life couldn't go on until I knew.

I awoke to a sound in the kitchen. At first I thought it was a cat moaning, but we didn't have a cat. I got out of Mama's bed and tiptoed into the hallway. Standing in the shadows, I peeked into the kitchen and saw Daddy sobbing. I was too scared to go to him, because he might say that Mama was gone. I didn't want to hear it, because that would make it real. I crept back to Mama's bed. I pictured her face, and her image became so crisp, it was as if she was in the room with me.

I looked into Annie Shipman's bathroom mirror, and next to my reflection, there appeared a pale face with thin cheeks and gray curls. I smiled and turned, but Mama wasn't there. I looked for her behind the shower curtain and in the cabinet under the sink. I wanted to go home and tell Daddy that I saw Mama, but that would have to wait. I didn't want to ruin the evening for Will. I needed to be a good girl. I splashed water on my face and went back to the kitchen.

Annie asked me again, if I was okay. I said that the wallpaper brought back some sad memories. She nodded and handed me another cup of hot tea and whiskey. I kept my back to the front hallway and its wallpaper, trying to pretend it wasn't there. I made an effort to join the conversation at dinner, and tried to forget I had seen Mama in Annie Shipman's bathroom.

For dessert, Annie served my pie. I didn't want any, but I watched the others eat. Ken took a bite and smiled at me. Annie said she had never tasted a pie like that. Will dabbed his eyes. I thought I would burst with pride. My pie was so good, it brought tears of joy to my husband. Everyone finished their dessert, and when Annie asked if anyone wanted another slice, Will said we had better get home.

As we put on our coats to leave, Annie asked me to come over for lunch next week. I said I'd love it.

On the way home, Will asked if I liked Annie.

"Sure," I said. "I don't like that house, though. It's too dark and old. It's spooky."

"Our house is older and a lot darker."

"But it's home."

"By the way, next time don't forget to put sugar in the pie. It was so tart it made my eyes water."

"You didn't see your mother a lot after she died, did you?" asked Angie.

"I saw Mama a few times. I was young when she died, and I was closer to Daddy. The cancer affected her brain, and sometimes she didn't know who I was. When I was very young, I thought she didn't care; that she didn't love me. Then it would pass, and she'd be herself until she forgot I was her daughter again. Years later, I realized it was just the cancer."

"A girl needs her mother."

"You think Claire needs me?"

"I think she worries about you."

"She thinks I'm a crazy old woman who talks to the dead."

Angie examined her hands.

"I think she worries about you, too," I said.

Angie shrugged. "It's weird that they had the same wallpaper as in your house."

CHAPTER 10

One night, Will burst into the kitchen. "A cow's in trouble. I got to call the vet." Benny just managed to get inside before the door slammed shut.

Will went to the phone, leaving a trail of snow and mud on my clean floor. He dialed a number, waited, and hung up. "Damn. He must be out on a call."

Will rushed outside again, with Benny at his heels.

I had been in the barn many times, but the smell still bothered me, and I had never done any work there. Will said the cows weren't used to me, so I should just sit and talk with him while he milked, and they would get accustomed to my voice.

The night was bitterly cold, but I resolved to help my husband. I was a farm wife, and it was about time I started acting like one. I put on rubber boots, the red pea coat I'd bought on sale last year, and a wool cap with a green pom-pom that had belonged to Daddy. It was snowing outside, and the flakes looked suspended in the air. I made my way to the barnyard, a large enclosure surrounded by tall stone walls right next to the barn. I opened the gate and went in. A spotlight from the barn cast the yard in dim light and shadows. Will was standing next to a cow and touching the underside of her belly. I stepped carefully on the frozen manure, but slipped and flailed my arms to steady myself.

"Go get me some shortening," said Will. "Bring the whole can."

I didn't know why he needed cooking grease, but I went inside the house, found a can, and brought it to Will. Benny followed me for the round trip. Then Will asked me to get some baling twine from the old barn. I went as quickly as I could. It was dark and eerie inside the old barn. I knew that some twine was hanging on a nail just inside the door. I opened it, reached in, grabbed the twine, and rushed back to Will.

When I returned to the barnyard, the heifer's stomach was moving in and out with exaggerated rhythm. Will's jacket was off, lying on top of a pile of frozen manure. One of Will's arms was bare, and his shirtsleeve and long underwear dangled down his back like a couple of tails. He slathered grease on his arm all the way up to the shoulder. He left a swath of brown in the can.

"Shouldn't we try to call the vet again?" I asked.

"Cow's been straining too long. If we don't do something soon, that'll be the end of it for both of them."

Will lifted the cow's tail and slid his hand into her behind. His wrist and then his arm disappeared into the cow. I had seen cows artificially inseminated before, and the man doing the breeding had put his arm way up there with a steel rod that contained the semen. This cow was way past that. I swallowed the bile rising in my throat. I was a farmer's wife, and I was going to help. Will moved his shoulder and pushed against the backside of the animal. I asked him what he was doing with his arm up the cow's ass.

"Trying to turn the calf."

The cow made a mournful sound. Will's right shoulder pressed against her rear as his left hand held her tail up. I wondered if he was going to shove his head up there, too.

"Easy, girl," said Will.

The cow arched her back and moaned.

Will said to give him the rope. When his hand came out, it held two cloven feet. The hooves were tan, and the legs were delicately crossed at the ankles. I could see a little bit of the calf's pink nose. I watched as Will tied the rope around the calf's legs.

"When the cow lies down, the calf should come out okay, if we're lucky."

The cow didn't lie down. She continued to push. With each push, Will tugged on the rope and released it when the cow relaxed. After one long thrust, the calf started to slide out. Will moved to catch it, but all he could do was break its fall. When the calf landed, a mixture of manure, dirty snow, mud, and afterbirth splashed onto my pea coat, my face, my hair, and Daddy's hat with the green pom-pom.

The cow sighed. The calf yelled. I swore. I could feel cold bits of manure on my face. I looked in horror at my new red coat and the brown smears covering it. The smell was so bad I could barely breathe.

The calf was limp, lying in the mud. Except for a white spot on its back, and another over one eye, it was all black. Will wiped the mucus from the calf's nose and mouth. It shook its head and looked around as if it was confused. Steam rose from the animal, and the little chest moved with each breath. The cow turned her head toward the calf and mooed loudly.

Will rested his hands on his knees. He picked up the calf's hind legs and looked at the belly.

"It's a girl," he said.

He picked up his coat. The cow moved to the calf and started licking her. The calf rolled onto her belly and tucked her legs in. Almost immediately, she tried to stand, but fell to the ground. The cow kept licking the calf's skin. The calf stood for a second, shook, and fell back down. A trail of afterbirth hung from the cow's behind, and Benny crept toward it, as if he was stalking a prey. Will told Benny to stay. The dog sat on his hind legs and continued to watch with unwavering eyes.

"I gotta finish milking," said Will. He tossed his jacket to me. "Take this into the house for me, will you Lil?" He picked up the calf in his arms and headed inside the barn, the cow following him with the slime rope trailing behind her.

I slipped several times before getting to the gate. My face was cold, and I was shivering in disgust. In a minute, I heard the low growl of the milking machine.

When I got inside the back hall, I undressed completely and left my clothes in a heap on the floor. The warmth of the house made the smell of the manure worse. I wanted to scream. I ran through the kitchen naked and went into the shower. I washed, dried myself, and then did it all over again. I put on Mama's robe and fuzzy slippers, and padded into the kitchen. I lit a cigarette, took a puff, and tapped the ashes into the large glass ashtray that had belonged to Mrs. Cook.

When Daddy appeared, I told him that I had shit in my hair and didn't know if I could live here anymore. The motor from the milking machine hummed high and then low.

I asked Daddy what I should do. Then I thought I was better off with Will than without him. A little dirt wasn't going to kill me. How was I ever going to get used to that smell? I took a long puff. I had helped Will save a cow and a calf, and that was something. I wondered if the coat would shrink when I washed it, or if dry cleaning could save it. I wondered if it would always smell of the barn.

I smoked another cigarette, cleaned the ashtray, and put it away. Will didn't know I smoked, and I wanted to keep it that way. He might not like me if he knew.

Will came in sometime later. He too, had taken his clothes off in the back hall. He came into the kitchen naked. Benny followed him inside. Will stopped when he saw me sitting at the table. Benny wagged his tail.

"Has somebody been smoking in here?" asked Will. He crinkled his nose and sniffed.

"There was shit all over me. It was disgusting," I said. I touched my hair with my hand.

"I'm sorry, honey. You helped save them."

"My coat is ruined." I don't know what had possessed me to wear anything nice when I had gone out to help Will. I would only wear old clothes in the barn from now on.

"I'll get you a new one."

I took Will's hand and led him into the shower. I forgot about my hair, my pea coat, and the stink as he pulled me to him in the waterfall. When he kissed the side of my neck, my mind glided away. I was with Will, and then I wasn't. I tried staying with him that time, but I couldn't. I didn't have any control. As I drifted over the farm, the cold didn't bother me. I floated into the clouds that looked white even in the dark. Blood and manure covered the snow in the middle of the barnyard, the place where I, Lily Phelps, had helped my husband save a cow and her calf.

When I became aware again, Will was out of the shower, wiping himself with a towel. "Dry yourself Lil, or you'll catch your death."

"Red smelled of fresh wood when he was working at the lumberyard," said Angie.

"Ed used to smell like that when he came in from his wood shop. He did a wonderful job fixing up my old house. He refinished the floors and put in new windows," I said. "He made furniture, too."

"I hated it when Red called me fat and ugly, so I told Ma. She said that was nonsense. She said Red thought I was pretty. He didn't want to say anything because it would just go to my head. Do you think it's normal for someone to tell you they think you're ugly when they really think you're pretty?"

"Not for a grown man."

Angie looked into the fire. "On my birthday last year, Ma didn't come home between shifts, as usual. She didn't leave a card or anything. I ate supper alone, did my homework, and went to bed. I was mad at her for forgetting my birthday. She was dating Red, and I thought she didn't love me anymore; that all the love she had for me, had gone over to him."

"That's not the way it works."

"Ma woke me up when she got home. She sat on the side of my bed and handed me a cake, and a package. Inside, there was mascara, blue eye shadow, and pink lipstick. She said it was time for me to have my own make-up and learn how to use it. We went into the bathroom. There in the middle of the night, while I sat on the toilet seat, Ma put make-up on my face, and we ate cake. It was the best birthday I ever had."

CHAPTER 11

When I told Will I was pregnant, he lifted me off the floor, swung me around the kitchen, and almost stepped on Benny. He said he was going to teach his son how to become a man and a farmer.

"What if it's a girl?" I asked.

"Then you can teach her how to become a woman, and I'll teach her how to become a farmer."

Will said taking care of the baby was my job. I told him he was old-fashioned, and that both parents should raise a child. He said that may be, but he had a farm to run, and as far as he was concerned, his wife was going to raise his kids, and that was that.

I knew nothing about babies, so I was scared. I had never even held a baby. I considered asking Belle what to do, but then she would see how ignorant I was. Besides, she would tell Will, and he would be disappointed. The farm was enough for him to worry about. I wondered if women were supposed to know how to raise children just because they were women. I had no idea what to do, no instinct, and no confidence. I knew how to care for the sick, but not the young.

I smoked a lot that summer. One day, I told Daddy how nervous I was, and I asked him how to take care of the baby.

He told me to be happy, and do what comes naturally.

When I turned to ask him what the hell that meant, he was gone. I guess Daddy thought I should know what to do, too. He should have remembered that I had never been around a baby in my life.

One evening, Will caught me on the steps outside the house with a cigarette between my fingers.

"Are you smoking?" Will asked.

"I just like the smell," I said. I stubbed the cigarette out.

"You shouldn't smoke when you're pregnant."

"I'm not smoking."

"Don't."

From that point on, I took my cigarettes across the road to the pasture. I sat on a rock and lit up. Sometimes Benny went with me.

Neighbors dropped by with clothes their kids had outgrown. Everything was clean, patched, and in every color under the sun, including green plaid shorts with yellow suspenders. They brought toys, most of them dull and scratched. John Stone brought over a black baby carriage that his mother had used when he was little.

I ran into Debbie in the grocery store. I asked her how Jeb was, and she said fine. She was pushing a grocery cart containing twin toddlers. She had put on at least fifty pounds since her wedding. I told her I was pregnant.

"I'm so sorry," said Debbie.

"Why?"

"Your body blows up like a balloon. You can't get comfortable, no matter what you do. When the baby comes, it hurts like nothing you can imagine. All you do is feed 'em and change diapers. I tell you Lily, I haven't had a decent night's sleep in two years."

I couldn't breathe.

"Get some sleep while you can, and congratulations."

I got into the truck and drove home, smoking one cigarette after another. Will was walking to the barn as I pulled into the driveway.

"I thought you were going to get some groceries," he said.

"I guess I forgot."

"Mom said she was absent-minded too, when she was pregnant with me."

Mrs. Ham came over the next day, carrying a playpen in one hand and a grain sack with something in it for me in her other hand.

"If anybody in my family gets pregnant again, they can buy a new playpen. This one's for you, Lily," she said.

Mrs. Ham shuffled across the kitchen floor in her construction boots, dragging the playpen. She put it down on Mrs. Cook's Oriental rug. "I heard you ran into Debbie yesterday. Don't listen to her. The birth hurts, but everybody gets through it. Besides, most women around here have their babies at home. You're going to the hospital. That's bound to make a difference. Just raise the baby like you'd raise a calf. Feed it, keep it clean, talk to it, and things should turn out fine."

Then she handed me the sack. I was delighted that someone brought a gift for me. I gingerly peeked inside, and saw two dead chickens, feathers and all. I yelled and dropped the sack on the floor. Mrs. Ham cocked her head back and cackled, showing all the spaces in her mouth where teeth had been.

"I can see you ain't quite a farm wife yet," she said. Then she went to the door and opened it. "Will," she yelled. "Get your ass in here and take care of these dead chickens, so Lily and me can cook 'em for your supper."

Mrs. Ham sat at the kitchen table with her legs spread wide and her dress hanging down between her knees. I offered her some brandy from a bottle that Belle had left in the cabinet. She drank it straight down and put the glass on the table with a bang. I filled it again. She sipped the second drink. I poured myself a cup of coffee.

Will came inside and took the sack, returning soon with the chickens dressed and ready to cook.

"I don't hold nothin' against you for not knowing what to do with them chickens," she said. "It takes a while to learn everything you need to know on a farm." She looked at me with one eye closed. "You don't know nothin' about babies either, do ya?"

That afternoon, while Mrs. Ham drank brandy in my kitchen and showed me her recipe for chicken and biscuits, she gave me the first of many lessons in caring for a baby.

She brought a doll so I could practice changing a diaper and wrapping it in a blanket. Another afternoon, we talked about why babies cried.

"Well, I always checked the diaper first, but my kids were usually hungry, and that's why they cried. Paul, my oldest, just wanted me to hold him." Mrs. Ham took a sip of brandy. "Sometimes, the babies get a fever. If they ain't too hot, give 'em plenty to drink, and keep 'em quiet. If they're real hot, have Will drive you and the baby over to the clinic."

"How much do you feed a baby?" I asked.

"They'll let you know when they're hungry, and when they're full. They're like pigs that way. You can't make 'em eat more than they want."

"What do I feed it?"

"You can buy formula at the grocery, but I nursed my babies. It's a lot cheaper, and you can't tell me that stuff in a can is better than the milk God put in your breasts."

My body changed every day. My belly got big. Eventually, even my shoes didn't fit. I was always hungry. Sometimes, my energy left me like water running down a drain, and I was exhausted for days. Sometimes I had the strength of a bull, and I cleaned house because I didn't know when I'd get to it again, after the baby came. I took long walks in the pasture with Benny and Daddy.

I went to a used furniture store and bought a wicker bed, bureau, rocking chair, and nightstand. I painted the furniture white, and had Will carry it upstairs to a little room that had a view of the barn and driveway. I painted the walls a light blue color, as I had a feeling about the baby.

When my belly got so big that I couldn't see my feet when I stood, we stopped having sex. Will was worried about the baby popping out when he was on top of me. Besides, the doctor said we should 'taper off.' I would go upstairs with Will after supper, and we would lie side by side. Will usually fell asleep while I talked, but I didn't mind. Without the expectation of sex, it was peaceful being in bed with him. I wondered if this was what normal wives felt: comfortable, relaxed, and happy to be in bed with their husbands.

Then the nightmares came.

I was in the old house. I was walking toward the kitchen, my eyes fixed on the dancing spoons on the walls. I stepped into the room and fell, because there was no floor. I fell through darkness for a long time, and then I woke up.

In another dream, the man with crooked lips and pinhead eyes chased me through the old house. I woke up in a sweat. I couldn't sleep afterward. I just lay in bed, trying to shake off the chill from the nightmare, and wondering if my dreams would affect the baby.

Around noontime on the second Saturday in August, Will came in from tethering a field of hay, where a machine tossed the grass up into the air, helping it dry for baling. He walked in with Benny, hooked his hat behind his chair, and sat down at the table. Will and Benny both had bits of hay on them. I filled Will's plate with food and sat next to him, nursing a cup of coffee.

"Aren't you going to eat?" asked Will.

"I don't feel like it."

"You sick?"

"I'm just not hungry."

"I've never known you to refuse food."

"I don't feel right."

"Let's take a ride to the clinic and check it out. Just in case."

"I thought you had to bale hay today."

"It's not ready yet."

"Okay. Let's stop at the store, too. We could use some bread and coffee."

When Will finished eating, we got into the pickup and drove toward town with the windows down, and the scent of fresh hay wafting in.

The doctor at the clinic sent us over to the hospital. An hour later, a nurse was wheeling me into a sterile-looking room and helping me onto a bed. There were leather straps hanging down from the sides.

"What are those?" I asked.

"Nothing for you to worry about," said the nurse, as she tied a surgical mask behind her head.

A contraction seized me, and the nurse looked at her watch. She stuck a needle into my arm. "Something to make you feel better," she said.

Soon, I couldn't make out faces any more, just general shapes and forms.

"Where's Will?" I asked. My body felt heavy, as if I was under a rock.

"He's in the Waiting Room."

"I want him in here with me."

"It's just not done, honey."

A fog came into the room. "Close the window," I said. "And go get Will."

A hand patted my shoulder. The fog entered my brain, and then nothing was clear.

In what seemed only seconds, a nurse was shaking my shoulder and handing me a package wrapped in a blue and pink striped blanket.

"What's this?" I asked. The room was dark. "Turn the lights on."

"It's your baby, silly," said the nurse.

"I don't remember having a baby." I wanted to go back to sleep.

"You're not supposed to remember, dear."

She put the package in my arms. I held it tight, because I was afraid I might drop it. It was a boy. He had a wrinkled forehead, pinched eyes, a mole on his left cheek, and a puffy face. He looked unhappy. I expected to see a miniature version of myself. His eyes were like Will's, but he didn't look like anyone in the family, not even Daddy.

Will came in and kissed me. "I'm proud of you," he said. "Ten fingers and ten toes?"

I nodded. "What should we name him?"

"How about Donald, after your father?"

"William will be his middle name then."

"Donald William Phelps."

"We'll call him Donny."

Will kissed me again and rubbed the back of his finger against Donny's cheek.

After Will went home to milk the cows, the nurse came in with Donny and asked if I wanted to feed him. I nodded. She placed Donny in my arms and handed me a bottle.

"Could you leave us alone?" I asked.

The nurse hesitated for a moment. "Sure. Let me know if you need anything."

I remembered what Mrs. Ham had told me about breastfeeding, so I decided to try it. As I took my arm out of the hospital gown, I thought of Will in the barn, squatting down to put inflations on each teat of a cow, the milk running into the hoses, through the pipes, and into the tank. My breast was swollen into roundness. I squeezed a nipple with my fingers. A drop of liquid oozed out. It looked like pus.

I rubbed a nipple against Donny's lips. I watched him decide what to do with the thing poking his mouth. I closed my eyes at the first suck, and when I opened them, I was terrified. Instead of Donny's fat cheeks, I saw the crooked lips, swollen nose, and pinhead eyes from my nightmares. The crooked lips were sucking my breast, and the tiny eyes were leering up at me. I couldn't breathe. My baby was a monster. I screamed but there was no sound. I snatched my breast away from the creature, and Donny started to cry.

I paused with my mouth open, and looked at Donny. I sighed in relief at the mole on the left side of his face, and the cherub cheeks, swollen from crying. I shuddered at the strangeness of what had just happened. I put my arm back in the sleeve of the hospital gown and called for the nurse.

"I'm awfully tired," I said. "Would you feed him?"

After she took Donny away, I curled up under the covers, shaking like I was out in a blizzard.

I was exhausted, but all I did was toss and turn. My mind churned as I tried to forget what I had just seen. When I finally drifted off to sleep, I dreamed that the man with crooked lips was calling my name as he chased me through the old house.

"Did that really happen?" asked Angie.

"I wouldn't lie to you."

"Pretty weird, Grandma."

"Do you ever have nightmares?"

"Sometimes. Ma says it's because I eat right before going to bed."

"If food caused my bad dreams, I would have had a much simpler life."

"I don't sleep well when Red's around. He's all the way downstairs in the back bedroom with Ma, but it's like the house is unbalanced when he's there. Sometimes I envy the way you live here in the woods, all by yourself. You can do what you want and go where you want. I think it's great."

"Living alone has nothing to do with your dreams."

"But nothing ever happens out here."

"You don't know the half of it, child."

"I could live like a hermit. I think it would suit me."

"You can't run away from life."

"Why not?"

"Life is a gift, and you shouldn't waste it. It took me years to learn that."

"You're so old-fashioned."

"Besides, when you meet the right person, you won't want to live alone."

"You met Grandpa Will and still had nightmares."

"That's because he had nothing to do with them."

CHAPTER 12

Ed gave me a cradle he had made, with three hearts carved in the headboard. I wondered if it was a suggestion as to the number of grandchildren he wanted. It was so heavy that I left it on the kitchen table. Will asked if he could move it for me, but I liked it where it was.

The day we got home from the hospital, Peggy dropped by to see the baby. I was still nervous from seeing Donny's face change. Each time I went near him, I braced myself for a shock, even though what I had seen was too strange to believe.

I took a deep breath and peeked into the cradle. It was Donny. I picked him up, and he began to cry.

"You're not going to break him," said Peggy. "Hold him like you're glad to be holding him."

"I'm glad," I said.

"Give him to me," said Peggy. "I'll show you how it's done."

I clutched Donny to my chest and twirled away from Peggy. He stopped crying.

"You see? You just have to hold him like you mean it," said Peggy.

I put Donny back in the cradle and sat down. Peggy poured coffee into cups, and I added brandy.

Peggy told me she was dating Sam Wheeler, the mechanic at Pip's Garage who had come to my old house to kiss me one night long ago.

"But you said you'd never date him because he drank too much," I said.

"I did, but then I realized I drank as much as he did, so it's okay."

When Will came in to eat that night, he leaned over the table and looked into the cradle. Donny cried. Will scrunched his shoulders and picked Donny up with two hands. The baby looked tiny in Will's arms. Donny fell asleep right away, and Will ate his supper while cradling the baby in one arm.

The second day home, Donny fell asleep after his breakfast bottle. In a few hours, he was awake again and crying. I followed Mrs. Ham's instructions. First, I checked the diaper. Then I tried feeding him. Finally, I took his temperature. It was none of those things, so I paced the floor, leaning him against my shoulder, while he wailed into my ear. Finally, I put him on a blanket spread over Mrs. Cook's Oriental rug. The moment I put him down, he was quiet. He stared up at the ceiling, where the chandelier cast prisms of light.

After a week of late-night feedings, early morning crying, and fearing what I might see whenever I looked at Donny's face, I asked Belle to take him for the day. After they left, I swept the floor, made lunch for Will, and went upstairs to rest. I closed the curtains and stretched out on the bed.

Maybe Belle could keep the baby for a few days, but it was my duty to care for my son. Besides, if Belle kept the baby, Will would know something was wrong. I imagined the look of disappointment on his face when I told him that I feared looking at his son. Will would send me away. He'd find someone else to care for Donny. I'd be all alone again.

I gave up on rest and went outside. Will was across the road, leaning on the gate to the pasture.

"Come boss, come boss." Will's chant broke the spell of quiet that hung over the pasture. The cows lifted their heads at the sound of his voice and turned toward home. Many formed a line, head to tail, as they meandered between the rocks and juniper bushes, along the narrow path that led to the gate.

I waited until the cows had crossed the road and were in the barnyard. Then I got into the pickup truck and drove toward Belle and my son. My hands were shaking as I lit a cigarette.

Daddy appeared, but I couldn't tell him that Donny had turned into a monster. Maybe something was wrong with me. Daddy vanished when I pulled into the driveway at the old house.

Belle looked up from the newspaper and smiled. The black baby carriage stood next to her Adirondack chair. The high-pitched hum from Ed's electric saw sounded like a far-off swarm of bees. I walked over to the carriage and braced myself. Donny's chubby cheeks moved as he breathed. He was asleep.

"Hi Donny," I whispered. His eyes fluttered open. He looked up at me and smiled. On that warm afternoon, with my baby smiling up at me, I knew I had to get through this somehow. I had to figure out what was wrong, so I could be a normal mother.

On the way home from grocery shopping, I stopped at the Shipman house to tell Ken to come by for a cow that Will wanted to sell. Donny was with Belle while I ran errands.

The trees along the Shipman's driveway covered the road with a roof of leaves. The cruiser was parked next to the barn. Ken must be inside. I was in a rush, because I had bought ice cream at the store, and didn't want it to melt before I got home.

I opened the barn door and stepped inside. A thick layer of dust and chaff covered everything, just like in the old barn at home. A rusty tractor was in the middle of the floor. Horse harnesses hung next to a collection of pitchforks, hoes, and shovels. Paint cans with drips of color on the sides were piled against the far wall, next to ladders, sawhorses, planks, and several cardboard boxes. The sun filtered in through the cracks in the door.

At the other end of the barn, there was an open door leading to a room. I could make out filing cabinets, the edge of a desk, and two long shadows on the wall. I walked toward the sounds of people talking.

"I don't want you here." I recognized the voice as Ken's. I wondered if he and Annie were having a fight. Another man spoke, but I couldn't make out the words.

Then Ken stormed through the doorway and stopped when he saw me. "What are you doing here?" He sounded angry.

I said that Will wanted him to drop by to pick up a cow.

Ken took me by the elbow and led me outside.

"Look, I'm sorry. I'll be there first thing tomorrow." He glanced back at the barn. "I'm in the middle of something."

I asked him if everything was okay.

He smiled and opened the door of the truck. I got in and started the engine. When I turned to say goodbye, Ken was gone.

I went looking for Will after I put the food away. He was in the milking parlor.

"Someone was with Ken today in his office at home, and he didn't seem too happy about it," I said.

"Who was it?"

"Not sure. It was a man though, from the voice."

Will told me that Ken's father was coming up from Florida, and maybe that's who was in the barn. He'd moved away when Ken was in high school.

"Ken's father was a painter by trade," said Will. "Sometimes on the school bus, Ken would talk about him. He never had a good thing to say about his old man. I've never heard a son talk that way about his own father."

"Why do some families hate each other, Grandma?" asked Angie. Her feet were on the coffee table, stretched toward the fire. She wiggled her toes.

"Just because people are related, it doesn't mean they like each other."

"Ma said that you and Uncle Donny had a lot of issues."

"What exactly did she say?"

"She said it was like you loved and hated each other at the same time."

"Claire doesn't know the whole story."

"Ma doesn't like it when I come over here."

"I'm glad you do. Family's important."

"I wish Ma felt that way. I wish she'd stop calling you crazy."

"I've had my problems."

"You don't seem crazy to me." Angie paused. "Do you think I'm going to go crazy one day?"

"Well, you have a lot of Grandpa Will in you, and he was the most level-headed person I ever knew. I think you're going to be okay." I hoped with all my heart that my words would come true.

CHAPTER 13

The face with the crooked lips and pinhead eyes that I had seen transposed on Donny's body stayed with me like a tattoo etched on my brain. I hardened myself each time I looked at my baby, expecting the worst. I would squint my eyes and steal a peek at him. If it looked like Donny, I opened my eyes. If it didn't, I ran into the bathroom, locked the door, and stayed there until I had enough courage to come out. In the months leading to Donny's first birthday, the face hadn't come back, and I dared hope it was gone for good.

One morning, I was in a rush. Ken and Annie Shipman were coming over for supper. I had to go grocery shopping and finish canning a batch of string beans from the garden. Mrs. Ham had shown me how to preserve vegetables, and I was getting good at it. I liked the idea of feeding Will and Donny from the garden all year long. I got the stove going to finish the beans. I had to wash the kitchen floor and dust in the living room, too. The place was never going to measure up to Annie's polished standards, but I had to try. I had no idea what I was going to make for supper.

As I fed Donny, I tried thinking of what Ken and Annie might like to eat. I could make meatloaf, Will's favorite, but it wasn't fancy. I could make a stew or roast a chicken. I dipped the spoon into the jar of mashed sweet potatoes, put it in front of Donny, and waited until he moved his mouth around it. He was sitting in his high chair, wearing a bib with the picture of a yellow duck.

When the sweet potatoes were gone, he kicked his feet, acting as if he was still hungry. I got a jar of pears from the fridge. When I came back, I noticed the unmistakable scent of a baby in need of a diaper change. I plopped the jar into a pot of water on the stove to warm and then carried Donny into the dining room. I put him on the table to change his diaper.

I held my breath as I opened the diaper to the brown mess that oozed around the little body. I lifted his ankles so his backside hung in the air a few inches above the table. After some broad swipes, I moved the dirty diaper to the side and put a new one in its place. I grabbed a clean cloth and wiped him in the cracks and crevices. I lifted the whisper of his sex and cleaned under it. The skin was soft, like a rabbit's foot.

Donny's face disappeared. The nose grew big, and the nostrils flared like they belonged to an angry bull. The pinhead eyes stared at me. The crooked lips bent into a sneer. The face from my nightmares was back.

Bolts of lightning crackled inside my head, and a raspy voice called my name. I screamed at the face, but it didn't make a difference. Big workman's hands reached out to me.

I ran into the bathroom and locked the door. As I leaned against it, trying to catch my breath, I heard Donny screaming and the raspy voice laughing. I wanted to save my son, but I was too scared to move.

I don't know how much time had passed when I forced myself to open the door, while praying that the man with the pinhead eyes was gone.

To my relief, Donny's little mole and fat cheeks were back. His face was red, and wet with tears. His voice sounded hoarse as he cried.

Thank goodness he hadn't fallen to the floor in my absence.

"I should never have come here." Angie jumped to her feet.

"You wanted to hear the story, so I'm telling you every blessed thing."

"Ma said you weren't right in the head. No wonder she doesn't want me coming over here."

"Let me explain," I said.

Angie ran out the door before I could say anything more.

By the time I got to the front steps, Angie's snowflake pajamas were barely visible through the trees and bushes along the road.

I wondered if I wanted to live or die. I decided I didn't care, but I had better damn well go get my granddaughter.

I rushed inside for my car keys. Angie was scared and confused when she had come over this morning, and I had made it worse. I had gone too far; had told her too much. I went outside, got into my car, and started the engine. I had lived a life of secrets, and now that I had told the truth, I wished I had said nothing.

I drove along the narrow road until I spotted Angie. I slowed to keep pace beside her.

"Please Angie, get in the car. Let me drive you home," I said.

She ignored me and kept walking.

"At least let me tell you why."

"I know why. You're sick." Angie wiped a tear off her cheek.

"I was sick, long ago, and I want you to know about it. Come on, Angie. Get in the car."

Angie stopped. She stood still for a long minute and then got into the car quickly, as if she didn't want to give herself a chance to change her mind. I drove slowly, until I was out of the woods, and then turned left onto the state road, toward Claire's house.

"Did you act that way with Ma or me?" Angie wiped her nose with the back of her hand.

I shook my head. "Something happened to me long ago."

"Okay."

"Okay what?"

"Tell me."

"I thought Claire told you everything already."

"I don't think she knows the whole story."

I tried to calm down as I finished changing Donny. I couldn't look at his face. I carried him into the kitchen and put him in his chair. I was exhausted and shivering. Somehow, I had to control that face, or control myself when that face appeared. Somehow, I had to keep from hating my son because of that face. I didn't know whether Donny was a twisted soul who had control over me, or whether I was going crazy.

I stood in the kitchen next to Donny's high chair, looking at anything but my son. He had stopped crying and was kicking his feet against the back of the chair. Then I remembered the jar of pears. The water was boiling. The pears would be too hot to give to Donny.

I rushed to the stove and moved the pot to the side. I held my hand over the water and felt the warmth. I looked at Donny. Pain might heal me and save him. I would do anything to save my son. I moved my hand closer to the boiling water and picked up the jar. I screamed as the heat scorched my skin. It drove away the memory of what had happened. White pain filled me like a cleansing snow. I held the jar for as long as I could. It shattered on the stove when I let go. Pieces of glass skated over the iron. Globs of mashed pear lay in miniature pancakes on the lids. Donny screamed. The kitchen filled with the smell of burning fruit. My hand throbbed. I sank to my knees.

Later, when Will came in for lunch and asked about the bandages on my hand, I told him I had burned it on the stove.

I called Annie Shipman and canceled our plans for dinner.

That night in bed, Will said, "I know how to make your hand feel better." He kissed my neck.

"Is that Donny whimpering?" I asked.

"I don't hear anything."

"My hand hurts, Will."

"You don't have to do anything." He kissed me on the mouth and moved his legs between mine.

I closed my eyes and tried not to think about the swollen face and crooked lips, but not thinking about it, made the image clearer than ever. Will had his arms around me. I felt myself drift away. Then the horrible face appeared on Will's body, and I clenched my hands into fists. A stab of pain shot up my arm. I was back in the bed.

I cried out.

"Oh baby," said Will. He moved faster in his rhythm, his breath heavy on my neck.

Will's face was back. The pain had driven the monster away.

Will bucked into me, slapping against my thighs. I kept my fist clenched as tight as I could stand. I cried out again in pain.

My entire arm throbbed by the time Will finished, and shifted his weight off me. He fell asleep right away, with his left arm draped over me. For a few minutes, I let him enjoy the rest I had given him. Then I gently picked his arm up by the wrist and moved it. Will turned over as I slipped out of bed. I put on Mama's robe and fuzzy slippers, and went downstairs where I found the bottle of aspirin. I took two, and sat in the dark kitchen smoking for a while. Then I went backupstairs to bed.

I became obsessed with that face, trying to remember why it was in my dreams. Was it someone my family had known? Was it a relative? I spent hours paging through an old album that Mama had put together before she got sick. I looked at the pictures of me, Mama, Daddy, and people I didn't know. I searched the photographs for men with white hair, crooked lips, and pinhead eyes. I looked at each picture with a magnifying glass, desperately searching for the face from my nightmares, and finding nothing.

I slipped into trances, thinking about that face. While I tried to remember why it terrified me, I didn't hear Donny's cries until they became a frenzy of screams. It was during those times that I was glad Will spent so much time away all day. He was in the barn early in the morning and in the evening. During the day, he was in the fields or working in the garage. If a cow was sick, or about to give birth, he stayed in the barn, sometimes well into the night. His absences gave me time to collect my energy and compose myself. Then, with Will watching me, I could pick Donny up and hold him for a few minutes, tilting my head down, and smiling as I diverted my eyes away from my baby's face.

One evening, Will surprised me by coming in from the barn early. He caught me sitting at the kitchen table with my head in my hands, wondering if I should tell him about the face with crooked lips and pinhead eyes. Will would never understand. He might send me away. He asked me what was wrong.

"Nothing," I said.

He said I looked tired, and we should go see the doctor at the clinic. I didn't want to talk to a doctor. How could I tell anyone what had happened? I couldn't even tell Daddy. I said I just needed sleep, and Will let it go.

The weeks became months. Sometimes when I looked at Donny's perfect little body, the monster face came back, and the raspy voice commanded me and tried to control me. When I heard the voice, I put Donny on the floor and ran out of the room. Sometimes I turned on the radio to let the music drown out the voice. Sometimes I sat in a corner, looking at the scars on my hand and screaming. Donny screamed, too.

I listened for the voice every second I was with Donny. I looked for the face with the crooked lips every time I changed him, every time I washed him, every time I even looked at him. When the face appeared, I screamed and ran away, leaving Donny alone and crying.

Thank God he wouldn't remember. He was too young to remember.

Early one October, I was at the stove, making oatmeal for Donny's breakfast. He was playing in the living room.

"Time to eat, Donny," I said.

He looked up from a battlefield of soldiers and tanks splayed over the rug. He got up and ran to the kitchen, but tripped and fell face first on the hard floor. There was a pause before he started crying.

I ran to him and picked him up. I expected to see the monster's face, but I had to know if he was all right.

"Are you okay?" I cringed at what I might see.

As Donny cried, he started to change. His lips went from red and plump to the crooked line that brought terror to my heart. His eyes shrank to black pinholes. I screamed and ran to the alcove in the kitchen that hid the door to the bathroom. I went inside and locked the door. At least he was crying and conscious, and probably not hurt.

I sat on the toilet, under the window with white lace curtains. His screams slipped into the room through the keyhole and under the door. I scratched at the burn scars on my hand until I drew blood, but the screaming didn't stop. I covered my ears with my hands and the screams were softer.

"Stop crying," I said, as I rocked back and forth.

Finally, I put my hands down. It was quiet. Donny wasn't screaming any more. I wiped my face with a tissue and blew my nose. I unlocked the door and peeked out.

Peggy was kneeling in the kitchen, with Donny's arms draped around her neck. His cheek leaned against her shoulder. He was smiling. He had the face of an angel. I straightened up and strode into the room. When Donny saw me, he wiggled out of Peggy's arms and ran away.

"He was crying," said Peggy. She stood and put her hands on her hips. "Why was he crying?"

"I made banana bread. Want some?" I went to the counter. My hands shook as I reached for the coffee can.

"Why didn't you take care of him?"

"He's alright. He tripped and fell just as I went to the bathroom. I couldn't wait."

"Have you been crying, too?"

I shrugged. "I'm feeling lousy. Might be something I ate."

"You poor thing. Sit down and let me do that." Peggy made the coffee. She drank two cups and ate half of the banana bread, while telling me that she and Sam Wheeler had had a fight. He'd spent the night sleeping in the field. "The dirt must have been easier on his back than sleeping in his truck."

After Peggy went home, Donny fell asleep, and I went out to the orchard to pick apples for pie. I tossed the bruised ones against the stone wall and put the good ones into the sack. I tried not to think about Donny.

After a while, the sack was full. I wiped away the sweat on my forehead, and I took a step toward the house. The face with the crooked smile, swollen nose, and pinball eyes was in front of me.

"What do you want?" I said. My head throbbed. "Who are you?"

My heart was racing. My skin was hot. I had to protect Donny. I picked up an apple.

Suddenly, I was under the bed in my old house. Liza my doll was on the floor, but out of reach. How was I going to save Liza? Shoes came into my room. They were covered in red and yellow dots that looked like little balloons. The heel on one shoe was red, as if it had stepped in some paint. The face with the crooked lips looked at me sideways, and a hand reached out to me.

"Come here," said a raspy voice. The hand grasped mine and pulled me out from under the bed. "So this is where you sleep."

I threw the apple at the face. The apple passed through the swollen nose and disintegrated against the stone wall. I grabbed another apple from the sack and threw it. Bits of apple flew into the air as it smashed against the wall. The scent of apple juice filled my nose. I took another apple from the sack and threw it, and another and another. The apples made a strange kissing noise as they passed through the face and hit the stone wall. I kept throwing apples at the face until the sack was empty.

Then the face went away.

None of this was Donny's fault. To make it up to him, I bought him the best toys I could afford, by taking money away from my grocery budget. I cooked his favorite foods from scratch. I made special treats for him.

I hoped that the gifts would be what he remembered.

As he grew, he spent more time outside, exploring. At first, I followed him because he was too young to be alone. He'd try to slip away from me. If I turned my head for any reason, he'd run away. Sometimes he laughed as he ran. It didn't feel like a game to me, though. It felt like he didn't want to be with me.

As he got older, I followed him, because I couldn't bear to be anywhere else. I constantly watched him, avoiding his face, but always aware of where he was, always prepared to protect him.

One afternoon, Donny ran out of the house. I ran after him, calling out for him to stop and let me catch up. He just kept running. I was halfway down the driveway when he slid under the gate to the pasture. Then he disappeared over the crest of the hill. I opened the gate and went along the cow path, past the trees, through the thistles, and around junipers, searching for him. It was as though the pasture had swallowed Donny up. I didn't know where to search next, so I went back to the gate, sat on a rock, and smoked a cigarette. I wanted to ask Daddy if he would help me find Donny, but he didn't come by that day. In a little while, Donny came back, and I followed him home.

As I finished talking, Claire's house came into view. The small two-story building that was in need of paint had housed four generations of my family, from me and my parents to Claire and my granddaughter. The little house was our family estate, ghosts and all.

"Red's there," I said. His pickup truck was in the driveway.

Angie slid down in the seat. Her feet were on the dashboard. "Let's go back to the cabin."

I was so relieved that I coughed to cover it.

"Don't let Ma see your car," said Angie.

I made a U-turn and hit the gas.

"I'll take you home whenever you want."

Angie stared straight ahead. Her forehead wrinkled, as if she was thinking about something.

When we got back to the cabin, I fixed us bologna sandwiches and a pitcher of lemonade, for lunch.

CHAPTER 14

"One night Will asked, "Do you like sex, Lil?"

My stomach sank. I couldn't tell him that I floated out the window, blocked sex from my mind, and wanted to scream every time he lay on top of me. "What do you mean?"

"You seemed to really like it at first, but now, I'm not sure," he said.

"Of course I like it," I said. I could explain that I liked him, but hated sex. He wouldn't understand.

"If there's anything you want me to do, anything you want me to touch or kiss, you'll tell me, won't you?"

"You do it just right."

"Just the same, if anything occurs to you, you'll let me know?"

"Sure, Will."

Donny wasn't in first grade yet, and Will was already starting to slow down. After supper, he napped in front of the TV. Then he went up to bed and actually slept most of the time, which was fine by me. The memory of that first night with him still shook me. While I cringed at the thought of sex, I got very good at blocking it out. I attributed Will's decline in interest to the fact that he was getting older. He no longer hopped out of bed in the mornings, and silver hair began to appear on his scalp. He asked me if he looked old. I said he looked good.

Four years after Donny was born, I was pregnant again.

When I told Will, he said it was a gift. I couldn't go through it all again, with another baby who turned into a monster. I held my face in my hands and sobbed. Will put his arms around me.

"I didn't know you wanted a baby so badly," said Will. "You're a wonderful mother." He wiped my eyes and kissed my cheek.

Over the next few weeks, all I did was pray for a girl. For some reason, I didn't think anything odd would happen if it was a girl. A girl would be like me. I could handle that. Whenever I thought the situation was hopeless and it was going to be a boy, I caught myself before sinking into despair. I pictured a little girl wrapped in a pink blanket, with pink booties on her feet, and waving a little silver toy. It made me feel better.

I didn't want to think about what I would do if it was another boy.

I wanted to do something special for Donny before the baby came, so I took some of the food money and bought him a set of building blocks. I spilled the pieces of colorful plastic over the flower petals woven into Mrs. Cook's Oriental rug, and waited on the floor for Donny to come inside.

After a while, the door slammed and Donny came in.

"Donny, come see what Momma got you." I said.

He came over, his eyes on the pieces scattered over the carpet. I showed him how to put them together and told him he could build anything he wanted. I put two pieces in the palm of my hand and held it out. Donny picked them up with two fingers. He didn't touch my skin. He clicked the pieces together and held them in his fist.

"Good, Donny."

Donny's eyes glistened. I would watch him from the kitchen as he played with his new toy. We would be happy. I was a good mother.

With the pieces still clutched in his fist, Donny ran out the door.

He was overwhelmed, I thought. I awkwardly got to my feet and went to the window as Donny disappeared into the barn. I imagined him sitting on a stack of hay, grateful, yet unable to say so. After all, he was just a little boy. I saw myself consoling him, hugging him. Oh, how I wanted to hug him. It would be the hug of a normal mother.

I went to the barn. Donny was taking slabs of hay from Will and tossing them into the feeding trough for the calves. Each time he took some hay, Donny paused and looked up at Will's face, as if to ask whether he was doing it right. They walked along the trough, father following son, distributing the hay, while the sun came in through the crevices in the walls. Donny glanced back at me without expression, as if he was looking at a pile of wood or a rock in the field.

The next morning, when I went into the living room, the blocks were gone. I went back upstairs and slowly opened the door to Donny's room. He was asleep, with the covers twisted around his legs and his mouth open wide. The plastic pieces were all over the floor, covering the rag rug in his room, in confetti of red, yellow, and green.

I ate all the time. I ate because of the fresh terror a new baby might bring. I ate because of the secrets I would take to my grave. I ate because I hated sex and still got pregnant. I popped slices of sandwich meat into my mouth, and drank from the cartons of orange juice in the fridge. I ate pies, cakes, maraschino cherries right out of the jar, ice cream, any kind of candy, and hazelnuts I had picked from the tree in the orchard. I ate because it gave me something to do besides worry about having another boy.

After lunch one day, I was in the kitchen with Daddy. Benny sat next to me, with his head in my lap. Donny was outside with his father.

"I'm real nervous about this baby," I said.

"What the hell for?" asked Daddy.

"Dunno." I couldn't tell Daddy what had been going on with Donny. It was too horrible to remember, let alone discuss. Besides, he might think I was crazy and disappear for good.

"You should be glad you're pregnant. Farms need kids to help with chores. After this one, why don't you have a few more?"

"Well if you want grandkids so bad, why don't you get pregnant?"

"You don't have to get all huffy about it."

"I'll get damn huffy whenever I want."

Mrs. Ham walked in. She never knocked.

"Who the hell are you talking to?" she asked.

"Nobody," I said. Daddy had disappeared.

"I talk to myself too, when the kids aren't around. I need to hear voices. It don't seem so lonely that way. Got any brandy?" Mrs. Ham's eyes lingered on Daddy's chair.

"How can you tell if the baby's going to be a boy or a girl?" I asked.

"If your skin is soft, it means a girl."

I breathed a sigh of relief. My skin was perfect. "What else?"

"If you crave sour food, it means a boy."

"What does it mean if you crave everything?"

"Twins," said Mrs. Ham, as she cackled and then drained the glass.

That afternoon, Mrs. Ham taught me how to knit. "It keeps your hands busy so you don't keep stuffin' food in your face. I gained sixty pounds when I was pregnant with Paul. I swear, knitting kept me from gaining a hundred."

My first knitted creation was a misshapen scarf, but I got better with practice.

I knitted a blanket, booties, a sweater, and mittens, even though the baby would have to wait a few years to use them. When I was sick of knitting, I smoked, but only when I was sure Will wasn't around.

I cooked plentiful meals for Donny, Will, and me. I made mounds of spaghetti, roasts with hills of mashed potatoes, and chicken and biscuits like Mrs. Ham had taught me. Despite all the food, I noticed that Will was still as thin as ever, but I was almost the size of the tractor. At least I had an excuse to be fat.

With Donny spending more time with Will, the boy seemed to be anywhere but with me, and that was probably the best thing for both of us.

One evening after supper, Will asked, "Are you happy, Lil?"

"Why wouldn't I be?" My stomach sank. Did Will suspect something was wrong?

"I know you're glad to be having another baby, but you seem tired and distracted. Are you okay?"

"Of course."

"Sometimes I think Donny's too much for you."

"It's being pregnant, that's all." I rested my hands on my bulging stomach.

"You'd tell me if there was something wrong, wouldn't you?"

I smiled and went to the counter to get Will a piece of cake. I cut an extra-large slice. Maybe if he was busy eating he wouldn't ask me any more questions.

"You know Mom could come over and take care of the baby for a while. She'd be glad to help out," said Will.

"I hate asking Belle. She's not young anymore."

"What about Peggy then? You never see her. Why don't you do something with her, and get out of the house for a day?"

"She's gotta work, and besides, she's still seeing Sam Wheeler. There's no way I want to take her away from him, even if it's just for a little while. Besides, I'd rather stay home and put my feet up."

"Okay, but no more chores in the barn. You've been helping me with the calves and cleaning up, but I want you to rest. I'll see if Ed can help me. It'll do him good to get out of that woodshop for a while."

"Good luck trying."

"You'll see. Things will work out." Will took a bite of cake and smiled. "Is there any milk?"

After the contractions and the rush of getting to the hospital, the baby was born. I was so relieved when the nurse said it was a girl, I cried. At least I wouldn't see a monster attached to my little girl's body, or I didn't expect I would.

The nurses smiled at my tears, wrapped the baby in a blanket, and put her on my chest. She wiggled into me as if I was a pillow. The baby didn't cry or pout. She looked comfortable and at peace with the fact that she had just been born. I moved the blanket away from her face and took a good look. Her skin was pink. The corners of her lips drifted gently into her cheeks, and it looked like she was smiling. The tip of her nose swept upwards, like a tiny pig nose. I resolved to name her Sissy, after a pig I had read about in a children's story.

From the start, it was as though Sissy knew what I was thinking. When I was sad, she seemed sad. When I laughed, she laughed. When I scolded Will in the spats that husbands and wives have, Sissy cried. She moved her head toward me when I came into the room. Her eyes were constantly on me as I moved around the kitchen.

As soon as Sissy could speak, she made high-pitched noises that called out to me, and acted as though I understood her special language.

As Sissy grew, she played with her toy broom when I swept the floor. She played with her toy oven when I cooked. She put plastic plates and cups on the little play table, when I set the table for supper. Sometimes, when I turned quickly at the sink or stove, I almost stepped on her as she was always at my side, neck extended upwards, mouth open, and a giddy smile on her face.

Angie picked up another sandwich and took a bite. I handed her a napkin.

"You and Aunt Sissy always got along," said Angie.

"Mothers are supposed to get along with all their kids, but it doesn't always work out that way."

"Like with you and Ma?"

"Claire and I didn't talk much. When we did, we fought. It was usually over important things, like dating, school, and marriage. In the end, she always did what she wanted."

"She had a right to make her own decisions, Grandma."

"At sixteen and about to ruin her life? Don't you think it was up to me to say something?"

"You think Ma ruined her life?"

"If she had finished high school and waited to find the right man before having a child, things would have been a lot easier. Back then, she was out of control. She wouldn't have listened to anybody."

"I ruined her life?"

"No, Angie. Having you saved her. You made her focus on someone besides herself. You're the reason she got up every morning. You gave her life purpose."

"And all I had to do was cry and poop." Angie looked toward the kitchen. "Is there anything else to eat?"

It was harvest time, and Sissy was walking, although she still preferred being carried. I was dressing her on the bed in the room with the white wicker furniture that overlooked the driveway. She stood with her arms in the air and her fingers wiggling like worms as I pulled a dress over her head. The sun gave the blue walls a heavenly brightness. As soon as the dress was on and her hands were free, Sissy put them in my hair.

"I make Mommy beautiful," she said.

I peeked out the window. Donny was walking to the barn. I stepped forward with Sissy in my arms.

Donny stopped and looked up at me.

Wrinkles flew across his forehead, and his lips twisted into a snarl. I stepped backwards. Could he possibly remember anything? He had been too young to remember. Boys go through times when they dislike their parents. This is just one of those phases. It had to be.

"Mommy. You're squeezing me. Hurts," said Sissy.

I relaxed my arms and moved forward to look out the window again. Donny was gone.

I took Sissy into Donny's room. I wanted to stretch out on Donny's bed and wait for him. We would talk and be normal. I would explain how I had protected him. But he would be angry if he saw me on the bed. He would tell me to leave. I wanted to be near his things: the desk covered with tiny gray plastic parts from a model airplane, his books, and his clothes.

"Why are we in Donny's room, Mommy?" asked Sissy.

I put a finger to my lips to quiet the little girl, and Sissy mimicked me. I sat at the desk and opened the lower right side drawer. I examined the contents inside and went to the next drawer. I read his papers. I reviewed old tests and homework assignments.

Surrounded by Donny's things, I remembered a man with the shoes that had spots on them like little balloons. I picked Liza up from the floor. Then the man took my hand. He led me downstairs to the kitchen. There was a sawhorse and boards set up like a table. The wallpaper Mama had picked out before she got sick was folded up like ribbon candy. Some was on the walls. Small, discarded pieces were on the floor. The wallpaper had pictures of dancing spoons. There was a pail of glue, brushes, and rollers on the counter.

I pressed Liza's head into my shoulder. I didn't know what was going to happen, but guessed it wasn't going to be good.

The man unzipped his pants.

"Grandma, no," said Angie. "You ran away, right? Tell me you ran away."

"At the time, that's all I remembered."

"So you didn't know what actually happened or who it was?"

"Not then."

"That must have eaten at you, not knowing."

"Will and the kids kept me grounded, which was a blessing. I didn't know whether I was remembering a dream, or a real event; not for sure. Every time a memory came back, it chilled me to my core. It was like I was standing on the edge of hole, and every time I looked down, it had gotten bigger."

"You can't blame yourself for anything that happened."

"I can't?"

"You were just a kid."

"So are you."

The week before Christmas, Will and the kids went into the woods to find a tree to decorate. Donny carried the hatchet. Will pulled the old toboggan behind him while holding Sissy in his arms. She was wearing her red coat and pink hat. Her arms were around her father's neck. Donny was in the front, walking with sure steps, as though he had something important to do. I made him wear the hat with earflaps so he wouldn't catch cold again. He seemed to be sick constantly that winter.

I watched them from the windows in the living room as they crossed the road and opened the gate to the pasture. The snow had covered the rocks and tree branches lying on the ground, making everything look fresh and new.

Will put Sissy on the toboggan and pulled her along. She dragged her mittens in the snow. She picked at pieces of the juniper bushes. She covered her head with her hands when clumps of snow fell from the trees.

I couldn't see them any more when they got to the woods. I lit a cigarette and paced in front of the window like a duck in a shooting gallery.

When they finally came into view, Donny was dragging the toboggan. It had a fir tree on it, and Will was carrying Sissy, who was eating snow from her mitten.

They came into the house in a rush.

"Mommy, we got a tree," said Sissy. She was out of breath before she even spoke. She put her arms around my legs. Her cheeks were cold, and she smelled fresh.

We moved Sissy's table and chair to the side, and put the tree in front of the windows. We put it in a stand that Ed had made from a block of wood, with two slats on the bottom for carrying, and a hole in the top where the base of the tree belonged.

"Why did you pick this scraggly old tree?" I asked.

"It looked lonely, Mommy," said Sissy.

"Oh. Well, then, I'm glad you brought it home so it could have Christmas with us."

We decorated the tree that evening, after Will came in from the barn. Sissy grabbed clumps of tinsel in her fist and threw it at the branches. Most of the silvery strands fell to the floor in tangled puddles. She hung a plastic robin, a piece of red ribbon, and several glass balls. Will lifted her up so she could put the snowman on top of the tree.

We opened gifts on Christmas morning, after Will came in from the barn. We watched the kids rip open each package, look at what was inside, and then cast it aside for another package. Sissy examined the wrapping paper with as much interest as the gifts.

I gave Will a box tied with red ribbon. He opened it and held up a pair of white trousers. He looked at me through the crotch.

"I got a feeling that Mrs. Bishop's going to have us over this summer," I said.

"Huh?"

"I ran into her at the post office. She was all dressed up as usual, and I told her I liked her scarf. She said she bought it because it had little German Shepherds embroidered on the material. Then I said I'd love to see her house. She said she'd have us over someday."

"That's why you bought me a pair of white pants?"

"I want us to be ready."

Will kissed me on the cheek. "Sure, Lil."

CHAPTER 15

When I learned I was pregnant with our third child, I worried again about having a boy. But I hadn't seen the monster's face in years. I dared to hope once again that it was gone forever.

This time, as my belly grew, I craved the outdoors instead of food. I spent time with Will as he worked in the fields, harvesting corn for silage that he would feed to the cows in the winter. Almost every day I drove to the field in the pickup, sat in a portable lawn chair, and sipped iced tea. I spread an old Army blanket out in the back of the truck, and Sissy played there, protected from the chaff, dirt, and the occasional hay bale. She brought different toys every day. Her favorites were crayons and a coloring book, with pages she energetically covered in scribbles.

Will drove the tractor that pulled the corn chopper, and behind it, a trailer with sides. The chopper broke the stocks and ears up into small pieces, and blew them through a chute into the trailer. When the trailer was full, Will drove it home and dumped the pieces onto a cement slab that looked like a miniature runway. Then he rode over the pile with the tractor, crushing the pieces of corn so they would ferment. Later, the silage would give off an intoxicating scent that smelled like hot whiskey.

As he drove, Will spent most of the time looking back at the machinery, although glancing forward at regular intervals. When he got to the end of a row, he made a sweeping turn over the stubble to change direction. At every turn, he waved at Sissy and me. We always waved back.

I'd been helping Will more and more with the farm. Every day, I washed the pipes, tank, sink, and pails in the milking parlor. However, my primary job was raising the calves. I heated milk on the stove in the house and poured it into empty soda bottles that I carried into the barn. When the calves saw me, they all yelled in their sweet, flat voices. I put a large rubber nipple on the bottle, put the end of the nipple in a calf's mouth, and inverted the bottle. Each calf stretched her neck upwards and sucked to her heart's content. When I pulled the bottle away, she grabbed a piece of my shirt or coat with her mouth and sucked on that. Even when they grew and could drink their milk and grain from a pail, their intense joy at feeding time never faded.

Will even named a calf Lily, because she was born on my birthday.

We thought Donny, who was almost seven years old, was interested in farming. He was spending time with Will and already knew a lot. He was easily winded though, and very thin. Sometimes I caught him resting on the stone wall. The doctor said his heart wasn't as strong as it should be, but he'd grow, and his heart should catch up to the rest of him. I didn't know if Donny would have the physical strength to be a farmer, and it worried me.

Sissy was different. She had to go into the barn with me when I fed the calves, because she was too young to be left alone in the house for any length of time. While I worked, she sat on a bale of hay just inside the door where I could watch her. Usually, Benny was with her.

Every day as we walked back to the house, she would say, "The stinky barn makes me want to puke, Mommy."

I knew she would never be a farmer.

One afternoon, I was making the iced tea and getting ready to go into the field when contractions started. The baby was coming.

I picked up the phone to call Belle and heard someone talking on the party line. I recognized John Stone's voice.

"John, this is Lily Phelps. I hate to cut in on you, but I think the baby's coming. I got to get hold of Belle right away. Can you hang up and let me have the phone?"

"Holy cow! Are you okay?"

"No, John. The baby's coming, and I need to use the phone."

"Where's Will?"

"Out in the field."

"I'll be right over."

I phoned Belle, and in five minutes, she and Ed were at the farm. By then, the kids were jumping on the furniture chanting, "The baby's coming, the baby's coming." I told Ed where Will was, and he took off in the truck to get him.

A few minutes later, John Stone walked into my kitchen.

I shooed the kids upstairs because they were making too much racket, and went over to the front windows to watch for Will. Then I saw the truck. Will was behind the wheel, and driving faster than I had ever seen him go. A minute later, he was in the kitchen.

John spoke up. "I'll take care of the cows. Don't worry about nothin'. Even in the morning. I'll get Ed to help me if I need him. You just go."

Will looked at John and nodded. Then like a firefighter rescuing a child from a burning building, Will scooped me up in his arms and carried me outside. The truck was already running and pointed down the driveway. He opened the door and deposited me on the front seat. Ed waved at us from in front of the garage.

"You're going to be okay, Lil," said Will. He slammed the door shut, ran to the other side, and jumped in. I saw him look in the rear view mirror and sigh, so I turned around, and there was Benny, with his tail wagging, standing on the back of the truck.

"Get down," said Will. He banged his hand on the outside of the door. Benny hopped down and stood next to Ed, with his head cocked to one side.

I was sweating from the excitement. The contractions were coming closer together.

"I'm gonna get you to the hospital before that baby comes, no matter what," said Will.

I gripped the dashboard with both hands as we tore down the road.

"Slow down, or the baby's going to pop out right here," I said.

Will didn't slow down. He honked at a car in front of us and swerved around it. I slid over to his side and then back again as the truck returned to the right lane.

"Cut it out!" I said. Another contraction came, and it felt like a giant hand was squeezing my pelvis. "The baby's coming, Will."

"Hang on, Lil," he said.

It was wet between my legs. Did I just pee?

"Stop the truck," I said.

Will pulled over to the side of the road. He put the tailgate down and spread out the old Army blanket in the back of the truck. Then he opened my door. As soon as I stood, liquid ran down my legs. My water had broken. He helped me lay down on the blanket. I looked up at the maple tree and the branches hanging over the truck. The leaves were a vibrant red. It was a beautiful day, just like when we were married.

"What if something goes wrong?" I asked.

Will slid the bale of hay that was in the back of the truck toward me, so I could lean against it.

"I know what I'm doin'," he said.

"No, you don't."

"This is just like having a calf, at least in principle."

He pulled my panties off.

A contraction the size of Willow Springs hit me, and I let out a yell. Will put a hand on my belly and stroked. "Easy girl."

"Stop talking to me like I'm a cow."

Will kept stroking my stomach.

"Get this thing out of me."

"Push, Lil."

"What in hell do you think I'm doing?" I needed Daddy with me. He would calm me. It would be okay if Will saw him this once, when I was having a baby on the back of a pickup truck out in the middle of nowhere.

"Daddy!" I yelled.

"I'm right here," said Will.

Another contraction came. "Daddy!"

Will squeezed my hand. "I can see the baby. It's got hair."

"What color?"

"Dark."

Another contraction came, and I thought my insides were coming out. There was a blast of pain, and then it was over. A high-pitched whimpering sound came from the back of the truck.

"It's a girl." Will put her down on the blanket next to my hips and took off his shirt. He wiped the mucus from the baby's mouth and nose. Then she cried in earnest. He tied off the umbilical cord with a piece of twine, and then clipped it with a pair of wire cutters from the glove compartment. He wrapped the baby in his shirt and held her against his chest.

"You alright?" he asked.

I could barely answer him, for I had no strength left. As I leaned against the hay bale, I let my legs hang over the edge of the truck like two strands of limp spaghetti.

"Let me see," I said. Will handed me the baby. Her little face peeked out from the cocoon formed by Will's shirt. Her eyes were squeezed shut. Her face was red and blotchy.

"Let's get you to the hospital," he said. Will carried me to the cab of the truck, while I held the baby. He kissed me before he closed the door. On the way, we went over the names we had talked about, and picked Claire, after Belle's mother.

"Ma told me she was born in the back of a pickup truck," said Angie. "I never believed her until now."

"It's true."

"Nobody was there to help you."

"Will was there."

"But he wasn't a doctor."

"Sometimes being with someone you love during a difficult time is enough to get you through it."

"When I get home from school, I make supper as quick as I can and then watch for Red's truck. If he comes over before Ma gets there, I slip out the back and hide in the shed."

"Does your mother know that you don't like being alone with him?"

"She knows I don't like him, but it doesn't make any difference."

"Why do you say that?"

"Because he's still around." Angie looked away.

I had a sense of dread, but if I pressed her, she might never tell me what was really going on. I had to bide my time until she was ready to talk.

CHAPTER 16

Raising Claire became a family project. It was time for Donny and Sissy to learn how to care for a baby. I was doing them a favor by showing them how to change her diaper, feed her, and burp her, just like Mrs. Ham had taught me. Donny became expert at certain things, like testing the temperature of formula by putting a drop on his wrist. Sissy was still very young, and saw it all as a game. Occasionally, I propped Claire up with pillows and let Sissy feed her while they peeped at each other like newborn chicks.

One morning, I had my coupons and sale flyers from the grocery store spread out all over the table as I worked on my shopping list. Claire was in the living room, sleeping in the black baby carriage.

Donny came in, along with a rush of cold air.

"Close the door," I said. I threw my hands on the papers to keep them from flying all over the floor.

Donny slammed the door shut. I cringed at the noise. Claire started to cry.

"Now look what you've done," I said.

Before I could get to my feet, Donny ran to Claire.

He dropped to his knees, crawled forward, and peeked at his sister from the side of the carriage.

"Claire-Claire," he said.

The crying stopped. Donny rested his arm on the side of the carriage and presented a finger to the baby. Her little hands grabbed it and her feet kicked up under the blanket. Claire pulled Donny's finger into her mouth.

"You were just in the barn. Are your hands clean?" I asked.

"Oh." Donny pulled his finger away and ran to the bathroom. The baby started to cry again. Before I could get to her, Donny was back, wiping his hands on his jeans. He knelt by the carriage and offered another finger to the baby. Then Donny sneaked his free hand under the blanket and grabbed Claire's feet. She switched from crying to squealing with laughter, as fast as an electric light brightens a room.

I was glad they got along so well, but I envied their closeness.

"Were Ma and Aunt Sissy close, too?" asked Angie.

"They were, and I think it was their salvation."

"What do you mean?"

"We went through some tough times, and I think they helped each other cope."

"Aunt Sissy doesn't come over very often."

"They have their own lives and their own families. Maybe when they're together, it brings back too many sad memories."

"Ma said families are important, and that's why she wants me to get along with Red. She said one day we were going to be a family."

My heart sank.

I was cleaning the kitchen when Annie Shipman phoned and asked if I could come over. I didn't know what she wanted, but I went. Before long, we were sitting in the Shipman barn on bales of hay, next to the stacks of cardboard boxes and cans of paint that were stacked along the far wall. Ken's father had died, and Annie wanted me to help her go through his things.

"I thought he was living in Florida," I said.

"He was, and he visited us a few times over the years. He never stayed long. Ken didn't want him around. I thought he might eventually move back up here, because he had kept all of his painting supplies in the barn. The last time he visited he was sick, so he stayed. He was with us for a few months before he died. Ken didn't want anybody to know, because he and his father didn't get along."

"We would have come to the funeral. Why didn't you tell us?"

"Ken didn't want me calling anybody. There wasn't a funeral to speak of. No visiting hours or eulogy." Annie brought a box down from the stack and opened it. "Ken had an awful fight with him just before he died. They were in the spare bedroom upstairs in the back, and I heard their voices all the way out in the yard. Ken called him a sick son of a bitch. His father was dead by morning. Ken found him. When he told me, he said it was about time he died."

I pulled out an old work shirt and held it up. It was torn at the elbows and stained with paint. I threw it on the trash pile.

"Ken mopes around all day now. Sometimes, I catch him in his office, and he's just staring at the wall. His customers are getting angry, because he's not taking care of them. Some are taking their animals to another cattle dealer. His deputy is covering for him, but that's not going to last forever." Annie pulled another box down from the stack. "I've never seen Ken act like this. I thought if we at least cleaned up his father's things, he wouldn't have to look at them every time he went to his office."

I reached into the box and pulled out a pair of old work shoes dotted with paint. I stared at them for a second, and then dropped them as if they were on fire. I'd seen them before. The barn disappeared as my cheek pressed against the cool floorboards under the bed in my old room. The door creaked open. Shoes covered with dots of red and yellow paint like balloons, and a swatch of red paint on one heel, walked into the room. They stopped beside the bed.

The man with crooked lips and a swollen nose bent down and pulled me out from under the bed. I picked up Liza from the floor and clutched her to me. He took us down the stairs and into the kitchen. He unzipped his pants and took out something that looked like a finger. "Look what I have," he said.

I was surprised that he had a finger in his pants. I wondered if Daddy had one, too. The man picked me up. My legs hung down and I kicked him, but he didn't seem to notice. I held Liza tight and leaned away from him.

He kissed my neck. His beard was rough and it tickled. "Stroke it."

I had to do what he wanted because Mama was sick and I was supposed to be a good girl. I put my hand around it. It felt soft like a rabbit's foot. It grew big in my hands. The man took Liza away and dropped her on the floor. I stared at the dancing spoons because I didn't want to look at the thing in my hands.

He smiled without really smiling.

He pulled my dress over my head and took off my panties. He told me to stand in front of him and spread my legs. He kissed my chest, and I didn't like it. He pulled at my nipples with his teeth, and it hurt. He put the thing from his pants between my legs. He poked and bruised me. I wanted him to stop. Then he moved it in and out. I screamed because it hurt. He pumped faster and faster. Then he pulled away, and his finger spit out vanilla pudding. It landed on a piece of the wallpaper that was lying on the floor.

Before I could run away, he grabbed me, and pulled me close to his face. I gasped.

"What's wrong?" asked Annie.

The man with the crooked lips was Ken Shipman's father.

"Lily." Annie was shaking my shoulder. "You look like you've seen a ghost."

"I have to go." I stumbled out of the barn.

Annie followed me. "Lily, come inside and rest."

"I've got to go."

"You're not well. At least let me drive you home."

"I'm sorry." I got into the truck and drove away. I went too fast down the dirt road, and only slowed when a rock slammed against the undercarriage. I thought something broke, but the truck still ran.

Halfway home, I pulled off the road and reached for a cigarette. I kept a pack hidden under the seat. I was shaking so badly, I had to put one hand over the other to steady myself to light it. I breathed in, as if the smoke had healing powers.

The cigarette smoke in the truck grew thick. I opened the window a crack. I had come face to face with my nightmare. I knew why I had mistreated Donny, why having sex was so strange and twisted for me. I should be relieved now that I knew who belonged to the face, but I wasn't.

As I exhaled, I thought of the little girl in a green plaid dress and white ankle socks, holding a doll named Liza. I wanted to tell her everything would be all right, but it was too late for that, because she was all grown up.

If I told Annie and Ken what I knew, Ken would lose himself in a bottle of whiskey. If word got out about his father, Ken might lose his cattle business. The town might vote him out of office. Even if I could muster the courage to tell them, I wouldn't, because of what it might eventually do to their marriage. It wasn't Ken's fault that his father was a bastard.

I wondered what Ken's father did to other children. I wondered if they had trouble having sex and raising children. I wondered if they saw monsters, and if they had learned somehow to be happy.

I wondered if he had done something to Ken. Is that why Ken hated him? I put my head in my hands and cried for all the children, for Ken, and for the little girl with the doll named Liza.

I wondered if I should tell Will. He might not want me anymore. He might think I was making up a story. But no, Will wouldn't think any of those things. He would just get angry at a dead man. I didn't want to make his life harder, so I decided to keep quiet.

I had a suspicion that there was more to the story, buzzing in my ears like an unseen mosquito.

The phone was ringing when I got home. "Why did you run off like that?" asked Annie.

"I don't feel good."

A few hours later, I heard the sound of an engine in the yard. I peeked through the window. Annie's red car was in the driveway. I ran down the steps to the cellar and hid like a thief, in my own house. A door squeaked open. Annie called my name. I stared at the underside of the kitchen floor as Annie crossed it, to the living room. The door to the hallway that led upstairs creaked open. "Lily, are you in the bedroom?" Annie crossed the floor again and stopped in the kitchen. Then a door closed with a thud. An engine started. When the noise faded, I crept up the cellar stairs. I opened the door slowly, as if Annie was going to jump out at me. I searched the kitchen and living room. No one was there. The car was gone. There was a casserole on the kitchen table, with a note from Annie saying I should bake it for thirty minutes, and she hoped I was feeling better.

CHAPTER 17

Just after the New Year, it snowed like the world was coming to an end. The barn gradually faded away, until it was barely visible from the house. Sometimes it disappeared completely in the gusts of white wind. Will and Donny shoveled the path to the barn each time they went to do chores or check on the animals. When Donny got out of breath from shoveling, I made him stay inside. All day, it seemed that Will didn't go anywhere without a shovel. Each time he came back into the kitchen, he was stiff from cold and covered with snow. Even Benny came in looking like a walking snow-dog. By evening, Will said it looked like it was going to snow for a good long while.

On day two of the storm, the milk truck driver phoned to cancel the normal pick-up. He said he would be there as soon as he could, but didn't know when that would be. I asked Will if he was worried, and he said there was enough room to store another day's milk. I thought of the large tank in the milking parlor and was sure we could wait out the storm. Nothing came down the road that day, not even snowplows.

On day three, it had stopped snowing, but the wind was still blowing and the drifts were enormous. The roads still hadn't been plowed. Will and Donny went into the garage and found the steel jugs that Ed had used to store milk in the early days, before buying the stainless steel storage tank with its fancy paddle that stirred the milk. They siphoned milk into the jugs to lower the level of the milk in the tank and put the jugs along the wall in the milking parlor.

After morning milking on day four, Will said, "Lily, the tank's full. We're going to have to start dumping milk. I don't know how much money we're going to lose. It could be a lot. It'll depend on the damn snow. Things are going to get tight for us." Will's voice trailed off.

Will's skin was gray and his eyes were dull. I sat him down at the kitchen table and poured a cup of coffee. It was my turn now to help in a significant way. This wasn't about doing chores. This was about saving paychecks. If we dumped milk, we would have to dump enough for an entire milking at once. That would be hundreds of dollars. If we could save the milk, we could save the money. We had no idea when the milk truck would get through. We might lose one milking, or we might lose ten. Will was exhausted. It was my turn to be strong and figure out how we could save the milk.

I called Ken Shipman.

"Ken, we need a plow to escort the milk truck out to the farm, or we're going to have to dump the milk."

"The graders can barely see where the road is, there's so much wind," said Ken.

"Isn't there anything you can do?"

"I'm only sending them out when it's life or death. It's just too dangerous. I'm sorry, Lily."

I hung up the phone and told myself it wasn't Ken's fault. Then I opened the door to the cellar. Benny rushed past me and ran down the steps. I went down and brought up every pot, jug, and container that Mrs. Cook had left behind when she sold the place to Belle and Ed. I scrubbed them in hot, soapy water. Sissy dried them. Claire placed them on the kitchen table. The kids brought the containers to the milk room, and Will filled them with milk from the tank. Soon, there were containers on every shelf and square inch of floor space in the milking parlor, but there was still too much milk in the tank and nowhere to put more containers.

"It's no use, Lily," Will said. We followed him into the house. Will fell into a chair and closed his eyes.

"I'm not going to let you give up, Will," I said.

There must be a way. I went into the living room and looked around. Then I began emptying the shelves on Mrs. Cook's bookcase. I piled the encyclopedias, the set of books written by Charles Dickens, and Will's agricultural magazines on the floor. When he realized what I was doing, Will came in to help. When the bookcase was empty, Will and I carried it to the milking parlor, careful not to scratch it as we maneuvered it through the doors and out into the cold, even though I didn't care. I thought the piece was hideous, and was glad to have it out of the house. We put the bookcase along a wall of the milk room, on the concrete floor, across from the pumping equipment. It filled the entire wall.

Will insisted we cover the shelves with brown paper bags from the grocery store, so we wouldn't stain the wood. Then we put pots full of milk on the shelves and stuffed coffee mugs in between. There was milk in vases, a lobster pot, a crock-pot, and the gallon jugs that Ed had used to store hard cider. We put milk in Mrs. Cook's fancy soup tureen, a whiskey bottle, oversized pickle jars, and soda bottles. We put everything we could on that antique bookcase that stood tall at the end of the room, its carvings of grapevines glowing in the white light coming in from the window.

On the morning of the fifth day, the wind had finally died down and the sun was shining. Will hadn't milked the cows yet, but there were no more containers. The tank was full. There was no place to put the fresh milk. We were going to have to dump from the tank.

"Wait until ten o'clock. The cows can wait until then," I said. I wanted to put off the inevitable. I was defeated. All the work to save the milk had been for nothing.

I stood at the stove stirring the oatmeal. I worried about how tired Will looked, the money we were going to lose, the bills we wouldn't pay, and the horrible waste. Benny lay at my feet.

In the quiet of the kitchen, there came the titanic blast of a horn. Benny jumped to his feet and I dropped my spoon. I ran to the front windows. The town grader, with its massive yellow plow, was muscling through the drifts, sending snow into the air like a mighty wind. Behind the grader was the milk truck, its long cylindrical body shining in the sunlight, and finally, the cruiser with its lights flashing, in a little convoy, making its way to the farm.

I dabbed by eyes with the dishrag as Benny licked the oatmeal from the floor. I threw on a coat and ran to the barn to help Will.

"I like it when families stick together," said Angie.
"We had to that winter, or we wouldn't have made it."

"If something bad happened at my house, I'm not sure Ma and I would stay together."

"Claire loves you."

"Last week, when I came home from school, I saw Ma's car and Red's truck in the yard. I was usually the first one home, so I listened through the screen door to find out what was going on, because if I asked, Ma might not tell me. Red was saying how those sons-of-bitches at the lumberyard didn't like him and made him look bad in front of the boss. He said that's what got him fired. Then Red told Ma that she should talk to her relatives down at the lumberyard and get him rehired. Ma said she had nothing to do with the business. It's her sister-in-law's family. Besides, she would be too embarrassed to ask. Then she said something else would turn up, it always does. Red said she didn't really love him, 'cause if she loved him, she'd help him get his job back. That's when he saw me. He told me to get my sorry ass inside the house. When I walked past him, he tripped me. I fell on my hands and knees, and it stung, but I didn't cry. I wasn't going to cry in front of him. He laughed and said I had clumsy feet. Ma was watching us and biting her lip."

"Has he ever hit Claire?"

Angie looked at me for a long second. "No."

"You sure?"

"No."

CHAPTER 18

In the summer, when the weather was dry, Will worked all the time. When he wasn't in the barn, he was in the fields baling, or getting ready to bale. He'd come into the house, have a bite to eat, and then go back into the fields. Sometimes, he didn't even start milking until eight or nine o'clock at night. Often, Donny and I helped him unload the trailer and stack bales in the old barn. I did most of the work, as stacking bales was hard on Donny. I started hoping for rain so Will could have a day off.

Late in July, I was in the kitchen with Daddy. It was so hot he had his shirt off. I was doing dishes at the sink, and keeping an eye on the kids outside. Sissy was in her oversized straw hat, trimming the rose bushes. Claire was playing tag with Donny, who was twisting his body from side to side to avoid her touch. When she finally tagged him, Donny turned around and tickled her. Claire laughed so hard that she fell to the ground. She rolled onto her back, hoisted her feet up in the air, and wrapped her arms around her stomach.

Benny jogged over and began licking Claire's face.

Sissy stood with her hands on her hips, as if telling the others to grow up. Claire's laughter reduced to a fit of giggles.

A dark cloud drifted over us, and soon it was pouring. The kids ran inside while the rain trickled in little rivers down the windows. The sound on the roof was like a herd of running cows. The rain stopped as quickly as it had started, and we ventured outside, to the sound of Will's tractor coming down the road. He looked like a wet rat perched on the seat between the two large tires. He parked in the driveway and as he climbed down from the tractor, said, "Damn day is shot to hell by that damn rain."

By then, the sun was shining again, and I suggested we go to the lake for lunch. The kids started chanting, "Picnic, picnic." Will nodded and smiled, as if he had no choice but to agree to the outing.

I made bologna sandwiches on white bread, and packed them in a sack with colas from the fridge. As an afterthought, I grabbed a ham bone that I was saving for pea soup and threw it into the sack for Benny. He deserved a treat, too.

I sent the kids upstairs to put their bathing suits on under their clothes, and had to yell at them to hurry up. They tumbled down the stairs and raced outside. Sissy went through the kitchen last, carefully jogging in her new white sandals.

We all piled into the truck. Benny climbed in the back. Donny straddled his knees on either side of the stick shift. Claire sat next to Donny, and Sissy sat on my lap, even though she wasn't the youngest. With the windows down and the kids chatting, we bounced along the road toward Moose Lake.

There were a few vehicles parked in front of the Rod and Gun Club, including Ken Shipman's cattle truck. Will said the bar must be open. We drove to one of the picnic benches on a grassy patch next to the shore. I opened the door of the truck, and Sissy carefully slid off my lap. She stood and smoothed out the wrinkles in her dress. Claire and Donny practically leaped out, throwing off their sneakers and clothes as they ran to the water. Benny went in with them.

Sissy slipped out of her dress, hung it carefully on a tree branch, and then tiptoed into the water. Will and I sat at a picnic table, clicked our cans of cola together, and watched the kids play.

"It's a good life," said Will.

Benny ran out of the lake, stood next to Will, and shook himself dry by spattering us with drops of water. I laughed. Will was right. It was a good life, and I was a lucky woman, even though I lived with a demon in my head and a load of guilt on my soul. The last time I saw the monster on Donny, he was four years old. He was taking a bath, and no one was in the house. I slipped into the room with him. I just wanted to be a normal mother and give my son a bath. Before I knew it, the swollen nose and crooked lips were back. I screamed. Kneeling beside the bathtub, with a washcloth in my hand, I screamed into my son's face and called him a monster. I ran outside and fumbled for cigarettes to calm my nerves. I was so disgusted with myself that I threw up into the bushes by the orchard.

When I tried to apologize to Donny, his eyes filled with tears and he ran away.

As Will and I sat on the bench, watching the kids swim in the lake, I touched the scar on my hand left by the scalding jar of pears. I remembered the face that belonged to Ken Shipman's father. I pinched the scar to stop remembering. I winced at the pain.

"What are you doing?" asked Will.

I brushed a drop of sweat from my forehead, stood, and rummaged through the sack. Will couldn't know what I was thinking, could he? I yelled for the kids to come in and eat. I tossed the bone to Benny. He grabbed it between his teeth, ran to a tree, flopped on his belly, and began chewing.

"Lil, why were you pinching yourself?"

"I'm so happy, I was making sure I wasn't dreaming." I cringed at the lie, but Will was smiling.

We ate the sandwiches and drank the soda. Will said we had better head back so he could check on the hay, to see if it was drying. As we drove down the road, Will suggested we stop for ice cream. The kids began discussing what flavors they were going to get.

"You like banana ice cream because that's what Jimmy Varney likes," said Sissy. She stuck her tongue out at Claire.

"I hate boys," said Claire.

"Do not."

"Do too."

"Girls," I said.

Frosty's was on top of a hill, behind a cluster of pine trees. We went up to a window to place our orders, while Benny sat next to Will, wagging his tail in the dirt. We got our cones and went over to a picnic table to eat.

"This is the best ice cream in the state," said Donny.

"Best in the world," said Will.

"In the whole universe," said Sissy.

Claire turned, put her cone down to the side, and let Benny take a lick.

"That's gross," said Sissy.

"Mind your own business," said Claire.

"Girls, stop it," said Will.

Claire started to laugh. "Stop tickling me, Dopey Donny."

"Don't call me that."

Finally, we were back in the truck and heading home.

"I'm going into the field to shake the hay before milking. If the weather keeps, I may be able to bale it tomorrow," said Will.

"Why don't I get the milking parlor ready for you in case you run late?"

"That would be great, Lil. Thanks."

Maybe doing more in the barn would help me. I could get things ready for milking every afternoon. All it took was putting the filters in place, turning some pipes, and filling tubs with water so the cows could drink when they came home. Besides, if I was busier, it might help me forget. I had a lot to forget.

CHAPTER 19

Angie snuggled under the blanket.

"Are you cold?" I asked.

"Comfortable."

"When I was thirteen, Daddy and I sat at Mama's bedside at the hospital. He said she was about to die, but I thought she was going to open her eyes, smile, and say she was fine. I never expected her to die, because she was my mother. When she passed, Daddy said that death came in threes. I wondered if he meant we were going to die soon, too. Years later, after Daddy died, he was more alive to me than ever. I didn't see much of Mama after she passed. Maybe it was because she got sick when I was young, and we never really connected, not like Daddy and me."

"You already told me how your mama and daddy died."

"This is different. I want to tell you about the year of three deaths."

No one knew Benny's age, as he was a full-grown dog when Will found him. Gray hair had recently popped out along the side of Benny's face. He ran less and slept more. He gained weight, and stood with difficulty.

One spring, Benny disappeared. It was so unusual for him to leave the vicinity of the barn that Claire begged Donny to go out looking for him. Donny went into the fields and came home just before dusk, with Benny at his heels. The dog looked cold, and his tail hung down between his legs.

Claire and I ran outside when we saw them coming up the driveway. She threw her arms around Benny's neck.

"He was just lying in the pasture when I found him. He seemed confused. I don't think he was planning on coming back," said Donny.

"You mean he went off to die?" asked Claire.

"You can't force anyone to live, Claire-Claire."

A few days later, Benny left the house again. Donny went outside to look for him, but he came back alone.

"Is he dead?" Claire asked.

"I don't know," said Donny.

Benny didn't come home that night. The next morning, I stood on the ridge and called his name, hoping he would hear me and come back to us. He didn't. Later in the day, Donny searched for him again and came home alone.

A few days later, we followed the kids out to the fence at the edge of the lawn, where we could see the pasture and the far hills. Benny was out there somewhere, under a juniper bush or next to a rock. The ground was wet, and the air was cold. Our boots made a kissing sound in the mud as we stepped across the yard.

Claire carried a bouquet of pussy willows she had found in the pasture.

"Good bye, Benny. We love you and we'll miss you." Claire threw a stem over the fence. It landed in the bushes below. She handed stems to Donny and Sissy, as they stepped to the edge of the lawn.

"You were a good dog, Benny," said Donny. He threw his stem over the edge.

"There will never be another dog like you," said Sissy.

Will and I stepped up to the fence and threw our stems down. "Sleep well, old boy," said Will.

We all waved at the pasture, five people standing in a line on the ridge at the edge of the lawn, making a gesture of farewell to our old friend. Then we went inside for milk and cookies.

That summer, I was getting ready to can tomatoes, when Belle called and said that Ed was dead. I moved my pots off the stove and got in the truck to get Will, who was cutting hay in the fields down near the old sawmill. I drove fast, as if it was vital that Will learn of his father's death immediately, as if time still mattered.

Belle was in the kitchen sipping a cup of tea when we walked into her house. She asked us if we wanted any, and Will said he could use a cup of coffee. I made some in the percolator. Will sat across from Belle and took her hand.

"How are the kids?" Belle asked.

"Everybody's okay," said Will.

There was no sobbing in that kitchen. As farmers, we were used to death. It came to people just like it came to animals: from illness, accident, or like Benny, from old age. Death was a part of things. No matter how sad you were or how bad you felt, you went home every afternoon to milk the cows and take care of the living.

"He was going to be seventy-five in a few weeks," said Belle.

I poured the coffee.

Belle said she had gone into the shed with Ed's lunch and had found him dead on the floor. He still held a chisel in his hand. His stool was on its side, and Ed was on his back, stretched out over the wood shavings. The tobacco in his pipe was still burning.

"I knew he was dead right away, by the way he looked. I'd seen enough of death in my day to know. I told him, how dare you die before me, you old son-of-a-bitch. I even had to blow my nose in my shirt because I didn't have no tissues." She took a sip of tea. "I called you two first, and then Ken Shipman, so he could get things moving with all that has to be done these days when somebody keels over."

Belle told us how she had gone to Maine with her sister a few years back, and had left Ed home for three days. She said it was lonely without him, even though her sister had chatted like an old crow. She said that loneliness was going to be a way of life from now on. I nodded. I thought about Daddy and how the dead can come back, but I didn't say anything.

We heard the sound of an engine in the yard. Ken was in the cruiser, lights flashing. Will went outside, then he and Ken went into the shed. An ambulance arrived a few minutes later, with a doctor I recognized from the clinic. Ken opened the shed door and gestured for the doctor to come inside.

Ed had built the shed after he retired. It had wood planks on the outside, and a stovepipe that looked like a crooked straw sticking up from the roof. He let the planks age, and when they turned a grayish-tan, he applied sealant to preserve the color. The windows had the same shade of grass-green trim that I had on my windows in the kitchen. The building looked snug and secure. The inside smelled of fresh wood.

Belle kept talking. "It surprised me when Ed got wrinkles and gray hair like everybody else. Sometimes, when I caught a quick glimpse of him, I'd ask myself, 'Who's that old man?' He always had his hair combed, always looked clean, even when we were shipping milk. I tell you, it's hard to stay clean when you work with cows, right Lily? Sometimes I think I married him because he was so clean."

I listened to Belle talk while I stood at the window. Will and Ken came out of the shed and leaned against the cruiser.

"Ed loved working with the wood so much that he smelled like a tree. He refinished the floors in the house. He made the coffee table, and the two rocking chairs in the other room. Took him an entire summer. He even built the kitchen table." Belle stroked the wood. "I wanted to cover it with a tablecloth to protect it, but Ed said no. He said he wanted to see the grain."

The doctor left the shed, walked to the house, and knocked on the door. I let him in. He told Belle that Ed was dead. Belle said she already knew he was dead, and if that was all he had to say, he should be on his way. The man mumbled condolences and left.

When Will went home to milk the cows, I stayed and made sandwiches. Belle put one on her plate and pinched at the bread, making a pile from the pieces.

"I wanted Ed to go into the furniture business when we got married, but he said he was just fooling around. Everything he made was beautiful, but he had a right to do what he wanted. He said farming was what he knew, so that's what he did. I think he was happiest though, when he was working with the wood." Belle turned her head to the window and Ed's shed across the road. "Can't be so bad dying while you're doing something you love."

Belle insisted on sleeping in her own bed that night. "I'm going to be alone from now on, so I better get used to it."

"I'm going home to take care of the kids, but I'm coming back and staying with you tonight," I said. I remembered how welcome I had felt that first time in her kitchen at the farm, when she put an old cardigan over my shoulders. This was the time for me to show her that I loved her.

I borrowed Belle's car and went home. I fixed hamburgers and fed the kids. I left three burgers on the side of the stove for Will, and rolls on the table with a plate of sliced cucumbers from the garden. I told the kids no fighting, brush their teeth, and be in bed by nine, or else. I went into the barn and told Will I was going to spend the night with his mother.

He smiled and said, "That's nice, Lil."

Belle had made up the spare room for me. She went into her bedroom as soon as I got there. I stayed up watching TV until the stations stopped broadcasting. Then I put on a sweater, went outside, and smoked, hoping that dawn would hurry up and get there. In the morning, I made a pot of coffee, toast, and two soft-boiled eggs. Belle was using a spoon to crack the shells when I walked out the door. I went home to make breakfast for Will and the kids.

The room in the funeral parlor had displays from the florist in town, and vases people had brought that were filled with treasures from home, including hydrangea, delphinium, iris, and geranium, in a quilt of colors. The room smelled like a garden. The coffin was at one end of the room, in front of a wall of curtains that went all the way down to the floor, making it look as though Ed was on a stage in a theater. There was a guest book on a podium near the door. A row of straight-back chairs was on one side of the coffin, for the family. Belle sat in one of the chairs, and I sat next to her. There were four more chairs next to us, for Will and the kids.

Ed had on his good suit, a blue striped tie, and a brand-new white shirt. His pipe was in his breast pocket, and his hair was slicked straight back. His face was tan, and he was smiling. He must have been smiling when he died. Will told me it was a heart attack.

The kids came in, walking stiffly. They slowed as they approached the coffin. They paused for a moment with their hands crossed and their heads down. Then they quickly sat down next to Belle and me. Will stayed near the guest book and talked to people as they came in. After a while, I let the kids go back outside.

I stayed with Belle at our posts, like stone lionesses guarding the dead.

Most people knelt at Ed's side to say a prayer and then went over to Belle, kissed her, talked a bit, and nodded to me. Mrs. Baleen came in with her husband and the twins, who were in their twenties and working in the warehouse at the Co-Op. Even Mrs. Bishop came to the funeral, looking like she just popped out of a catalog. She wore a white shirt, a dark suit, and a scarf with pictures of dogs woven into the material. She took Belle's hand. "I'm so sorry. He was a good man," said Mrs. Bishop. "You'll have to come over to the house for supper." Mrs. Bishop smiled at me as she passed by. I wanted to ask her if I was invited too, but I didn't think it was the right place or time.

People told stories about Ed that I had never heard before. Mr. Robbins talked about the year of the drought, when the well at their shack went dry. He and his wife had six kids, none past grade school. Mr. Robbins had gone to Ed with an empty milk container, asking for water.

"I hated to ask him 'cause water was scarce all around, and with all those animals, we knew it was tough for him in particular. But we didn't know what else to do, especially with the kids. We thought maybe he could spare just a little," said Mr. Robbins. He wore a dark suit that could have fit a man twice his size. His face was tan and heavily lined. "Ed filled up the milk carton with water, and we went on our way. Then a few hours later, a truck pulled into the driveway. It was Ed, with two milk cans full of water. He left 'em on the step outside and said to bring 'em back in a few days, and he'd fill them up again. Twenty gallons. It made Mrs. Robbins cry when she saw it, rest her soul. Ed said it was for the kids. I'll never forget it."

I had never paid much attention to Ed, or even Belle. They always seemed old to me. I had no idea that people outside the family loved Ed.

No one cried at the eulogy except the kids, and they tried not to show it, wiping their eyes and noses with their hands and refusing tissue when it was offered. Will said a few words about how he was grateful to have a father who knew both patience and love. Will's voice cracked when he said he was trying to be that kind of father to his own kids. When he finished talking, Will stood at the podium, staring at the door. I turned to see what he was looking at. A thin rim of light glowed under the dark pine doors, as if the sun was trying to push its way inside. Will wiped his eyes with a handkerchief and sat down.

Everyone came over to the house afterward. I put out cold cuts, bread, potato salad, macaroni salad, and a plate of sliced cucumbers. The girls had made cookies: chocolate chip, oatmeal raisin, and sugar. It had taken them an hour to arrange them on a platter. I made fresh coffee. Will put cans of beer and bottles of whiskey on the counter.

The men stood next to the liquor, helping themselves. The women filled plates with food, went into the dining room, and sat at the table under the chandelier that I had cleaned the day before. I had taken each piece of crystal down, washed it in ammonia and warm water, dried it, and put it back up. My arms were still sore, but the light fixture sparkled. The girls went from room to room together, never more than a few inches of space between them. Donny stayed near Will.

Mrs. Ham said she used to get all her gossip from Ed, before he retired and left the farm. When people stopped on the road to let his cows go by, they told him what was going on in town.

"He knew who died, who was born, and who was in jail. He knew every piece of machinery that was for sale within ten miles. He knew who had good cows and bad cows. He knew everything. He would have made one helluva reporter. He could of writ a whole newspaper by hisself," said Mrs. Ham, before popping one of Annie Shipman's deviled eggs into her mouth.

The guests left early to take care of their animals. Will refused an offer from John Stone to do the milking. Will said that taking care of the cows would help take his mind off his father. I didn't know how being in the barn would help him forget, because Will and Ed had spent so much time there together. Maybe Will wanted to go into the barn so he would remember.

After all the guests left, Donny went into the barn to help Will. Claire went in later, to help them clean up. After I put the food away and washed the dishes, I went outside behind the woodshed with a cigarette. I leaned against the building and took a deep breath. I closed my eyes, waiting for the feeling of calm.

Four weeks after we buried Ed, I woke to the blast of gunshots. It was light outside, and Will was already in the barn. I jumped out of bed and ran to check on the girls. They were still asleep. Donny was in the hallway. He had jeans on and was buttoning his shirt.

"What's goin' on?" he asked.

I shrugged and ran downstairs, with Donny at my heels. We threw on our boots and rushed outside. We saw Will walking toward us, from the cellar of the old barn, with a shotgun in his hand. He walked past us without saying a word.

Will went into the kitchen and opened the door to the broom closet. He put the gun on the rack above the top shelf, where it belonged. Then he sat down at the table. Donny sat across from him.

I put on a pot of coffee.

We sat in silence while the coffee perked. I poured some into cups, stood with my back against the stove, and waited for Will to say something.

Will's words were abrupt when they came, and they felt like hot water scalding my skin. He said that the floor under the calves in the old barn had collapsed in the night, and a dozen animals had fallen to the cellar below. He found the hole and the broken animals when he went in to milk. Most of the calves were already dead. He relieved the ones who were still moving with a gunshot to the head.

"All my babies are dead?" I asked.

Will nodded.

Donny asked if we should call Ken Shipman and sell him the veal. Veal always goes for a good price.

"I don't sell dead meat to the slaughterhouse," said Will. "Besides, Ken won't take animals unless they're alive."

"Can we eat the meat?" asked Donny.

I shuddered at the idea of eating my little friends.

"The animals fell fifteen feet to a hard surface. Their bones are broken and their guts ruptured. The meat is contaminated," said Will.

He drank his coffee all at once and left the room. Minutes later, I heard the hum of the motor in the milking parlor. I told Donny he could stay home from school and help his father. Then I woke the girls, fed them, and got them out the door in time for the school bus.

After the girls left, I usually went into the barn to feed the calves. I wouldn't have to do that today. My face was wet. When I had first started taking care of the calves, Will had warned me that they weren't pets. We might sell some, and others might die.

"Just don't get too attached," he had said.

Don't get too attached to the little pink noses that rushed to me every day. The calves fell into rapture when I fed them, as though nothing in the world was as wonderful as the warm milk and bits of soft grain that passed into their mouths. Sometimes a calf butted me with her head, unaware of the bruise it would produce. To me, this was an expression of joy. Don't get too attached. Will hadn't told me how to do that.

I wiped my eyes and wondered how the loss would affect the business. We raised the calves to replace cows that got too old or fell behind in production. We'd have to buy new calves to replace the ones we lost. Will would have to fix the barn floor. He would have to buy lumber, unless he cut down the trees himself and started up the old sawmill. That would be a lot of extra work though, and he might need to buy a new blade. Blades cost money, too.

I had lost twelve little friends.

Later that morning, Will parked the tractor and trailer near the barn's cellar. He and Donny loaded each of the twelve bodies onto the back. One held onto the front legs, and the other onto the back legs, and then they swung the calves onto the trailer, as if they were loading sacks of grain. Donny stopped and sat down. He looked tired and sad. It seemed like everybody was going to miss those calves.

When all the calves were on the trailer, they drove the tractor in the direction of the pasture and the woods.

A few days later, one of the cows had a calf. It was a girl. It felt good to have a little one to raise again.

When I thought about it, maybe Daddy was right. Maybe deaths came in threes, if you counted twelve calves as one.

"We never got another cat after Boots ran away. I wanted one, but Ma said she needed some time to get over him. Then Red showed up. I guess Ma forgot about Boots after that, but Red was no pet as far as I was concerned," said Angie.

"Will didn't want another dog after Benny died. Will saved Benny's life, and no other dog could replace him. Fate had brought them together, and it was a special friendship."

"Will you ever get married again?"

"I haven't been asked."

"If you met someone and he asked you to marry him, would you consider it?"

"Life's too short to turn love away, but I can't imagine myself being with anyone but Will."

CHAPTER 20

Donny collapsed in the lunch line at school and was rushed to the hospital. Days later, after Will and I had brought Donny home, we were sipping coffee at the kitchen table, when there was a knock at the door.

"Mr. Wilkie," said Will. "Come on in."

"Have a seat," I said. "How are things at school?"

"Kids will be kids," said Mr. Wilkie.

He ambled to a chair. His suit reminded me of a burlap sack. It took all the energy I had to get a cup from the cabinet. I had stayed at the hospital while Donny was there, napping in a chair next to his bed at night. When he came home, I lay awake, listening for any sound to draw me to his room like a magnet to metal. During the day, I went up and down the stairs with trays of food. I brought Donny books and magazines. I did everything I could to make him comfortable, like I had done for Mama and Daddy years ago.

"So what brings the high school principal all the way out here?" asked Will.

"Wanted to check in on Donny. How's he doing?"

Will said that Donny had a mild heart attack, but he was getting better and stronger every day. He said that Donny's grandfather had died of a heart attack, and it might just run in the family. Will said we were lucky it happened when Donny was young and strong enough to survive it. Besides, Ed had lived until he was almost seventy-five, so that was a good sign for Donny.

I made a face at Will, not believing that there was anything lucky about Donny almost dying.

"Mind if I smoke?" asked Mr. Wilkie.

I nodded and breathed in. I wanted to smoke so badly, I almost grabbed the cigarette out of Mr. Wilkie's hand, but I didn't want Will to know that I smoked.

Mr. Wilkie told us that Donny had been in the lunch line with the other seniors when it happened. "It was right after gym class. All of a sudden, Donny put his hand to his throat, stumbled forward, and grabbed the boy in front of him. The boy stepped aside, and Donny fell to the floor. The Hurley girl screamed, and that's what caught our attention so quickly. I think she likes your Donny. Mr. Simons, the gym teacher, got to him first. Poor man just exhausted himself breathing into your boy. Donny was pale as a ghost. We thought he was going to be the first boy to ever die at school."

Mr. Wilkie smiled. I wanted to slap him.

"We had to keep the kids away, 'cause everyone was pushing and shoving, trying to see what was going on. We got the kids out of the cafeteria. They lined up along the hallway and out the front door, like they were at a parade." Mr. Wilkie took a sip of coffee. "When the ambulance boys came inside, it got so quiet you could hear a pin drop. I don't think that's ever happened before, that you could hear a pin drop in that place. Like I said, everybody thought Donny was gone. Girls were crying, even some boys were wiping at their eyes, trying not to show how upset they were. But Donny made it. Boy, was he lucky."

I considered throwing the coffee pot at Mr. Wilkie's head. Will put his hand over mine.

"It turned out okay. He's okay, Lil," said Will.

The doctors told us that Donny had a weak heart and needed to stop exerting himself.

At night, as I sat up in bed listening for Donny's voice in a whimper or a sigh, I wondered if I had somehow caused his illness. Maybe it didn't matter that Ed had died of a heart attack. It was the way I had raised Donny and all the stress I had caused him.

Donny got better. His color came back. One morning, he got out of bed and came downstairs while Will and I were having breakfast. A white trumpet vase full of pussy willows from Mrs. Ham was on the table. She had brought it over for Donny.

"What are you doing out of bed?" I asked.

"Doctor said I could get out of bed this week," said Donny.

"Want something to eat?" asked Will.

"You need to get back to bed," I said.

"The boy said he's feeling better," said Will.

"I don't care. Get to bed!"

"I'm sick of bed. I want to have breakfast down here today, and I want bacon with my eggs," said Donny.

"You can't have bacon. Doctor said so," I said.

"Lil, ease up. He can have a slice of bacon and eat it here with us if he wants to. It'll do him good," said Will.

"What if he has another attack?"

"He can't spend the rest of his life in bed."

"Oh, yes he can!"

"The boy can do what he wants from now on, and that's the end of it," said Will.

In two weeks, Donny was taking short walks and doing a few light chores in the barn. In a month, he went back to school. He already had his license, so he started using the pickup truck on Saturday nights. He said he was going over to a friend's house. I thought he was visiting a boy in town.

Then one Saturday evening, on his way out to door, Donny asked me for some money for the prom. I was washing dishes in the sink.

"Sure. Who are you taking?" I asked.

"Cathleen Hurley," said Donny.

"I didn't know you liked Cathleen."

"We've been out a few times."

"When?"

"Saturday nights."

"I thought you went to see a friend in town."

"I did."

"Don't you think I would have liked to know you were dating a girl?"

"It's no big deal."

"Why did you lie to me?"

"I don't need your permission."

"Then I'm going to the dance, too. I'm sure they need chaperones."

"I don't want you going."

"What if you have another attack? Who's going to help you then?"

"If I have another attack, I'll be dead, Mother."

Donny left the kitchen before I could think of what to say.

As I drove up to the school on prom night, the first thing I noticed was the brightness. So many lights were on that the school looked like an outpost of day in a dark night. I parked the truck in the side lot and walked up the steps to the front door. Decorations were in the lobby and along the hallway, creating a tunnel of miniature mermaids and cardboard chests overflowing with plastic gold. I followed the decorations to the gym. The walls were wrapped in blue and green tissue paper, crinkled at the top to look like sea foam. Construction paper fish hung from the ceiling and the windows. The effect was childlike, amusing, odd, bright, dazzling, curious, and appropriate. The theme, Underwater Fantasy, was on a sign hanging from the wall. On a table near the stage, there was a box wrapped in pink paper to hold the voting slips for prom queen, and another box wrapped in blue paper for prom king. A band called the Buzzards had guitars and amplifiers set up on the stage. Tables and chairs formed a U-shape around the edge of the gym. I stood behind the refreshment table, along with three other mothers who were catching up on gossip.

Half a dozen teachers were there, lined up at the doors, smiling at the kids as they entered. The female teachers wore print dresses and necklaces. The male teachers wore striped shirts, blazers, and dress pants.

The girls wore long dresses, except for one, whose hemline went way above her knees and drew attention from everybody. Their hair was piled on top of their heads and decorated with silk flowers and ribbons. The girls looked older from a distance, but up close, their wide-eyed expressions gave them up as the youths they were. The boys wore dark pants and tuxedo jackets in white, yellow, and light blue. One jacket was a muted pink. In general, bow ties matched the color of the jackets. Some boys had jackets that matched the color of the gowns their dates wore.

Some kids sat in groups around tables, while a few couples sat alone. Girls floated to the restroom in pairs. Boys who came stag stood to the side, their heads turning back and forth as they watched couples on the dance floor. From time to time, they leaned their heads toward each other to say or hear something, without redirecting their gazes.

Then the lights went low for a slow dance. I walked over to a corner where I could watch Donny and Cathleen from the shadows. Spotlights made soft circles on the floor. When the lights fell on Donny's white suit, it glowed. Cathleen's wide taffeta skirt hugged Donny's legs. The space between them melted away. Donny made a small movement toward Cathleen's face. She tilted her head upwards, and they kissed.

"You're too young for this, Donny," I said.

The music was loud, and Donny didn't hear me. I snuck outside and smoked three cigarettes. When I came back inside, the dance was over.

"I'm not going to go to my senior prom," said Angie.

"You should. It's the first time you get dressed up for dinner and dancing, aside from weddings."

"I don't have a boyfriend."

"Why don't you ask someone to go with you? I'm sure there are plenty of boys who would be glad to be asked."

"They'll laugh at me because I'm fat, and Red says I have clumsy feet."

"You aren't fat, and don't listen to Red. He can't even hold down a job."

"I don't have anything to wear."

"We'll go shopping."

"Ma would have a fit if she saw me in a long dress."

"Your Aunt Sissy dressed up every chance she got. Sometimes she got dressed up for no reason at all."

"I'm not Aunt Sissy."

"Next time she comes out to visit, we'll all go shopping."

"Even Ma? I don't think she'll go."

"Then you, Aunt Sissy, and I will go."

"If it's around prom time, maybe we'll look at dresses."

"Of course."

"Do you think I'll ever get married?" asked Angie.

"I don't see why not. You remind me a lot of your Grandpa Will, and he made a wonderful marriage."

"How am I like him?"

"You both have a sense of humor. Will tried talking me into giving him a discount at the Co-Op, and you gave your mother a raw egg to eat on Easter morning. You both work hard. You're both very loving. I think any man would be lucky to have you."

A week after graduation, Will was at the supper table with the girls when Donny came in.

"It's about time you came inside. Go wash up. Your dad's waiting for his dinner," I said.

When Donny got back, I had the food on the table, and Will was cutting into his ham steak.

"I got something to tell you," said Donny.

"So tell us," I said.

"Cathleen and I are getting married."

My jaw dropped.

"You're awfully young, Son. You sure about this?" asked Will.

"Her father's going to give me a job at the lumberyard."

"They knew before we did?" I asked.

"If things go well, maybe I'll be helping Cathleen's father run the business after a while."

"You can't do anything strenuous, so how are you going to work at a lumberyard?" I asked.

"All I have to do is keep track of pickups and deliveries."

"I think it's great," said Claire.

"Well, if you love her, then you should marry her," said Will.

"I do, Dad." Donny sat down, put a spoonful of mashed potatoes and another of peas on his plate, mixed them together, and took a bite.

"Can I get a new dress for the wedding?" asked Sissy.

How could Will think that Donny was better off marrying this Hurley girl than staying home with me? I was too angry to speak. Will and Donny were ganging up on me. I ate while the girls chatted about the wedding. Then I went up to bed, waited for Will, and planned what I would say.

Will finally came upstairs.

"What were you thinking?" I asked.

He sat down on the bed. "He's got a weak heart, Lily."

"That's the whole point. He needs to stay home where I can look after him. How do we know she can take care of him? What if he has another attack?"

"Cathleen's parents think she's old enough to get married."

"Well I don't. Why are you all against me?"

"We don't know how much time he has left. We should let him get married."

"If Donny stayed home with me, I could make him live."

The day of Donny and Cathleen's wedding was clear and bright. We got up early. Everybody helped with the chores except Donny, who stayed in the house and got ready. He offered to go into the barn, but Will said no. He said every man should have a few days off from chores, and his wedding day was one of them. Even Sissy went into the barn, although she took such a long shower afterward, we were almost late for the ceremony.

Belle came over with a basket of blueberry muffins, and had coffee waiting for us when we got in from chores. With her silver hair, and in her silver suit, she shone like a dime.

While the girls were getting ready, I sat in the kitchen wearing the yellow satin dress that Cathleen had picked out for me, and watched Will help Donny with his tie. Will was talking in a low voice, no doubt telling Donny the secrets to being a good husband. I wondered if Ed had the same talk with Will on our wedding day. Donny looked happy and excited about his future, but I knew I was about to lose something valuable that I would never get back.

When Cathleen entered the church, everyone stood. There was no gust of wind driving her forward, like at my wedding. There were no garden trellises or dime store decorations, only fresh flowers and white ribbons. Cathleen floated down the aisle, holding her father's arm. She didn't look pregnant, thank goodness. At least they didn't have to get married, or so it seemed. Donny was handsome in his black suit, but as thin as a stalk of corn. I took a tissue from my pocketbook and wiped my eyes.

The reception was at Beckett Farms in Four Rivers. There were pink tablecloths in the dining room. Guests had a choice of chicken or steak, and waitresses served all the food. Belle didn't have to kill any turkeys. Annie Shipman didn't have to arrive with a beautiful cake and powdered sugar in her hair. Over the shrimp cocktail, I decided that I would go home with Will, when he left early to milk the cows.

The newlyweds rented a small house in town, with two bedrooms and a potbelly stove in the living room. Within a few years, they had a baby boy who they named Theodore William, after both their fathers. They called him Theo for short.

"Do you see your cousin Theo often?" I asked.

Angie was leaning back on the sofa with her eyes closed. "He comes by sometimes when he's home from college. But he's usually busy working at the lumberyard during break. Cathleen says he's going to run it one day."

"I'm glad you keep in touch. You're an only child, so your cousins are important. He reminds me so much of your uncle Donny that sometimes I forget it's not him."

Angie patted the back of my hand.

"Does Theo ever ask about me?" I said.

"He says he doesn't know you very well."

I chewed my lip and picked up the vase on the coffee table. I rubbed its soft, white curves. I didn't see Theo often, and the visits were always brief. I wished we were closer.

"That's a pretty vase," said Angie.

"When Mrs. Ham gave it to Donny, it was full of pussy willows."

"Is she still alive?" asked Angie.

I shook my head and began the story.

There was a fire at Mrs. Ham's house some years ago. It burned so quickly, there was nothing left by the time the fire trucks arrived. She was home with Paul. The Fire Marshal said he had been smoking in bed. Neither one made it out. The day after the fire, I drove over to Mrs. Ham's house. I sat at the picnic table in the yard and lit a cigarette. In a few minutes, Benny appeared. I hadn't seen him in some time. He jogged around the property, finding things to sniff among the charred rubble.

I sat there next to the remains of the house, and remembered all the things Mrs. Ham had done for me. I dabbed my eyes with a tissue.

"I'm going to miss you, Mrs. Ham," I said.

"Well I'm gonna miss you, too, Lily. Where ya goin'?"

I looked up, and there she was, in all her toothless glory, sitting next to me at the picnic table. Paul appeared too, next to Benny.

"I was wonderin' who'd be by today," said Mrs. Ham. "Debbie and Jeb came yesterday with their grandkids and there was a lot of commotion with the little ones runnin' around. You're the first to see me. Truth is, I don't know if the others will ever see me."

"What's it like being dead?"

"I guess it's alright. I'm not quite used to it. I don't have to eat any more, although I never minded eating. It's funny though. It's like I'd just drift away if I didn't force myself to stay put. I don't know where I'd go if I drifted, so I don't think I'll try it yet."

"You know I see my daddy."

"He had the cancer."

"Daddy visits me all the time. He won't tell me where he goes when he's not with me. He won't talk about being dead. Why is that?"

"Just 'cause you're alive, you don't necessarily know how life works. Same way with bein' dead. You have to kind of figure it out as you go along. Maybe he doesn't have any answers."

"I don't think Will sees his father."

"I really liked Ed. Once he told me how he went deer huntin'. He didn't want to shoot nothin' 'cause deer were such pretty things, but he went 'cause he was a man, and that's what men did. He was up in the woods by Shadow Pond. He leaned his gun against a tree, lay down, and took a nap. When he woke up, there was a deer not ten feet away, eating leaves from a bush. Ed said if he had a rope, he could have slipped it around her neck, brought her home, and used her to pull the plow come springtime."

"I see animal ghosts, too. Like Benny."

"That's interesting."

I turned my head away to light a cigarette, and when I looked back, Mrs. Ham, Paul, and Benny had all vanished.

CHAPTER 21

With Donny spending part of Christmas Day with Cathleen's family, I didn't know how much time I would have with them, so I thought a good lunch might entice them to stay. I had been cooking all morning. I got milk and butter from the fridge, added them to a pot of boiled potatoes, and mashed until the potatoes were creamy. I had a taste and wondered if the food in heaven could possibly be better. The roast ham gave off the scent of cloves and the holidays as I moved it from the oven to the side of the stove to stay warm.

As I took plates down from the cabinet and set them around the table, I thought back to Christmases at home when I was little. Every year, Daddy and I carried our presents into Mama's room and dumped them on the sickbed. Daddy brought in a small tree and put it on the chest at the end of the bed. Mama didn't want us to leave it there, so we just brought it in for a while. I made a plate of sugar cookies with red and green sprinkles on top and put them on the nightstand. No one ever ate them, but I made them every year anyway. Mama smiled when we opened the gifts. She always said the present I got for her was her favorite. She never wavered on that, even when the dementia kicked in and she asked me who that strange man was in her bedroom, as she pointed at Daddy. When she got tired, we tiptoed out, taking the packages, paper, cookies, and tree with us. We went into the living room. Daddy sat in his chair, lit a cigarette, and decorated the room with a garland of smoke. It hadn't mattered that Christmas was brief. At least we had something to remember.

The back door opened, and Cathleen came in holding the baby. Donny followed her, carrying gifts in his arms. He barely said hello before he put on his boots and headed toward the barn, where Will was milking.

Cathleen gave me a kiss on the cheek, wiggled the baby out of his snowsuit, and sat at the table with Theo in her arms.

"The baby's getting big," I said. I went into the living room and yelled up the stairs to the girls, saying Donny and Cathleen were here.

They came down in a rush.

"Where is he?" asked Claire.

"He went into the barn to help your father finish up," I said.

"He'll smell like cow poop when he comes in," said Sissy. She made a face and bent to pinch Theo's cheek.

While the girls fussed over the baby, I sat back and took a good look at Cathleen. I didn't know whether she expected me to be a mother or a friend, and we hadn't had enough time together to figure it out. She seemed to be a nice girl, though. I hoped she was taking good care of Donny.

Will and Donny finally came inside.

"Is Mom here yet?" asked Will.

"Belle wanted to go to church at noon. She'll be over later this afternoon," I said.

Will popped a piece of ham into his mouth. "She's going to miss one heck of a meal."

We went into the living room to open gifts. Will and I sat on the red velvet sofa. Cathleen put the baby on my lap. Everyone else sat on the floor. Claire took the presents from under the tree and slid them over the carpet to their new owners.

Theo was a beautiful baby. His skin was pink and covered in tiny white hairs.

Donny saw me gazing at Theo and watched me suspiciously.

Cathleen opened a package from Sissy. Inside, there were hairpins with fake blue sapphires. Cathleen tucked them into her curls.

Donny opened a box covered in two different types of wrapping paper. He pulled out a tie and draped it around his neck.

"It's for when you get promoted to the front office," said Claire.

"The lumberyard doesn't have a front office, and nobody wears a tie. Ever," said Donny. He poked Claire in her side, and she giggled.

"Well, you'll add some class to the dump," said Claire. Then she turned to Cathleen and smiled.

"I agree. My father's office is a dump," said Cathleen.

The baby started to whimper. I sniffed at his midsection. "Theo's got a load in his diapers. I'll change him for you." I stood up with the baby in my arms, and then walked toward the kitchen and Cathleen's diaper bag.

Donny jumped to his feet and snatched Theo out of my arms. The baby started to cry.

"I'll take care of it." Donny carried Theo into kitchen.

I followed them. Donny pushed the dishes aside, opened the diaper bag, and took out a plastic pad. He lay it on the table and put Theo down in the center. He started taking off the baby's diaper.

"Let me help," I said. I stretched my arms toward Theo.

Donny pushed me away. His touch felt like cold steel against my skin. Something was horribly wrong. There was anger in Donny that I had never seen before. He was always aloof, but that was his way with me. It was how he showed me he loved me. Maybe there was a problem at home with Cathleen. I knew that woman wasn't good for him. He and the baby should come back to the farm and live. He should let Cathleen fend for herself in that shack they were living in. I should never have let him get married.

"It ends now," said Donny.

"What ends now?" I asked. Was he talking about Cathleen? Maybe he was leaving her. Maybe he was talking about me. Maybe he was mad at me. Why would he be mad at me? I was a good mother.

"I love him. I love you," I held out my hand so he could see my burn scar.

"I know what your love is."

I gasped. Donny remembered what he wasn't supposed to remember.

"I was trying to protect you," I said. It was hard to breathe.

"Protect me from what?"

"From me." My hand flew up to cover my mouth, as if to stop my secrets from coming out. I commanded myself to speak, and tell my son that I had been abused, and had done everything I could to avoid abusing him. I wanted to tell him about the crooked lips and pinhead eyes that I had seen on his body, and how it had terrified me. I wanted to tell him how I couldn't look at him when he was a baby because I might see that face. I had to protect him from that face. I had to tell him my secrets and make him understand.

All I managed were sputters and grunts. I yearned for Donny to reach out his hand to me through the bitterness that hung in the room. I would grasp it, hold it over my heart, and never let it go. It was my time to speak, but I couldn't. I couldn't tell him I was a good mother. I couldn't tell him anything. I couldn't find the words.

"I was abused!" The words were out, and I was free. Things would be okay. Donny would understand. His anger would vanish. He would look at me with love in his eyes.

I waited for Donny to say something.

He was dressing Theo and acting like he hadn't heard me. I had to say it again. I needed to explain. Where were the damn words?

Cathleen, Will and the girls came into the room.

"What's going on?" asked Will.

"We have to leave," said Donny. He roughly squeezed the baby into the snowsuit. Theo screamed.

"Don't go," I said.

"Stop that. You're hurting him," said Cathleen. Donny zipped the snowsuit in one savage motion and put the baby in Cathleen's arms. "What's wrong, Donny?"

Donny jerked his head toward the door.

"We just got here," said Cathleen as she tried to comfort the baby.

"Your parents are waiting. We got to go."

Cathleen looked at Donny with a confused expression. "I'm sorry," she said, as she turned to Will and me.

Donny put his jacket on and draped Cathleen's coat over her shoulders. His eyes looked down as he closed the door behind them.

I ran outside in time to see Donny's truck going down the driveway. I ran after him, slipped on some ice, and fell on my face. By the time I got up, the truck was gone.

I jumped into the pickup and drove to Donny's house. I parked across the street and waited, even though I knew they wouldn't be home for hours. I lit a cigarette and told myself that I would knock on their door when they got home. I would go inside, sit at the table, and tell Donny my story. When the cigarette burned down, I lit another, and then another.

Daddy appeared through the smoke.

I told him about the day he went to the hospital, and I stayed home.

I told Daddy what the man did.

I wanted to ask Daddy if he would have killed the man, if he had known, but I didn't think so. Daddy had been too weak and sad to do anything. I told Daddy how I had to pretend with Will in bed, when his touch made my skin crawl. I told him how the horrible face had appeared on Donny's body, and about the voice that sent needles into my head. Donny hated me because I had tried to be a good mother. Ashes and cigarette butts overflowed the ashtray and fell onto the floor. I had to remember to clean up inside the truck before Will saw the mess.

I told Daddy that the man was Ken Shipman's father.

I decided to tell Will everything. Then I would tell Donny and Cathleen. It would be easier if Cathleen was there. Maybe Will should tell them, instead of me. Yes, Will should tell them. The girls wouldn't have to know, at least not right away. Will could tell them later. He would know what to say.

The smoke in the truck made me dizzy. It was so thick I couldn't see Daddy any more. I reached into the pack for another cigarette, but it was empty, so I drove home. When I got there, Will was in the barn. I went up to bed.

I forgot to empty the ashtray.

The next morning when I woke up, my eyes felt like they were full of sand. I would talk to Will today. After breakfast, we would take a ride in the truck, and I would tell him everything. Afterward, we would go to Donny's house and talk to him, together.

The phone rang. I rolled over to Will's side of the bed and picked up the receiver.

It was Cathleen.

"Donny had a heart attack last night. He didn't make it." Cathleen's voice was so soft, I thought I was talking to a child.

"Who is this?" I asked.

When I finally understood the message, I dropped the receiver, and Cathleen's sobs fell to the floor.

I put on Mama's robe and fuzzy slippers. I went downstairs and out the door. I walked across the driveway and into the barn. The air was cold in my lungs.

Will was inside.

"Lily, you got your slippers on," he said.

"Donny's dead."

The days of gray began.

CHAPTER 22

Donny couldn't be dead. He was too young. He had too much living to do. He had a child to raise. He was my son.

I went back into the house, got dressed, and waited for Will. When he came in from the barn, his eyes were red.

"Let's go to the hospital and see Donny," I said.

"Lil, you don't want to do that."

"Don't be silly. He's not dead. Can't be."

Will didn't argue. He went upstairs to change his clothes, but he was gone for too long. It occurred to me that he was talking to the girls. I wanted to shout up the stairs and tell him not to say anything, because Donny was okay. But my body wouldn't leave the chair. When he came back down, he picked up the phone and dialed a number. He said, "Hi Mom." Then he said that Donny was dead. I didn't know why he was upsetting Belle for nothing. Will asked her to come over and stay with the girls.

Will didn't talk on the drive to the hospital. He gripped the steering wheel with both hands and looked like he was driving to his own funeral. When we got to the hospital, we went over to the counter.

"May I help you?" asked one of the nurses. Her white dress glowed.

"You look like an angel," I said.

The nurse smiled.

"I want to see my boy, Donny Phelps."

The nurse looked at a chart and then at Will. Will nodded. We followed the nurse down the hall, into the elevator, and down into the ground.

The nurse left us outside a double door with frosted glass. She opened the door several minutes later and motioned for us to come inside. The room was big and seemed very clean. It was cold. The lights were dim. A metal table was in the middle of the room, and on it, a figure covered in a sheet. The nurse moved the sheet away. I was surprised that the face was so still. Donny always moved, even when he was asleep. His eyes twitched or his mouth curled.

Will gasped and turned his head away.

"This isn't Donny," I said. "This boy's dead." I touched the arm, and it felt cold.

Will took me by the shoulders and moved me toward the door. He nodded to the nurse.

"Get a blanket for that boy. He must be cold. It's so cold down here," I said. Will took me outside and helped me climb into the truck.

During the ride home, time changed for me. Each second became an hour, and each hour stretched to the length of a day, giving me plenty of time to realize that the boy under the sheet was Donny.

When we got home, I went up to bed and stayed there. I heard cars come and go in the driveway. I heard voices from downstairs. I recognized Will, Belle, and the girls as they spoke, the sounds drifting up to me. I didn't get out of bed.

Will made me get up on Wednesday, because it was the day of the funeral, and he said I had to go. I didn't want to go. If I didn't see Donny dead in the coffin, maybe he wouldn't be dead. On the way to the church, we passed houses with Christmas wreaths on the doors. I remembered that New Year's Day was close. Donny wouldn't go to any parties this year or any year.

It seemed a long drive to the church. Maybe Will didn't want to go, either. All he said during the drive was that the girls were with Belle. It wasn't until then that I realized I hadn't seen them in days.

The church was crowded. People squeezed into the pews and stood along the walls all the way up to the front. Two large displays of poinsettias stood on each side of an altar that was covered with a white cloth, the embroidered cross perfectly centered on the side facing the mourners. The sun shining through the stained glass windows cast circles of light onto the floor. The room was very still, as though Donny's death had made it unnecessary to speak.

Cathleen sat in the front pew on the right, with Theo in her arms. She wore a black hat with a brim that hid her face. Her parents sat on either side of her. Will and I were across from them on the left side. There was a white coffin in the aisle. I tried to keep my eyes away from the coffin. Sissy and Claire sat next to me. Claire was crying. Belle sat on the other side of the girls. Peggy was at the end of the pew, wearing a hat with so many feathers, it looked as though something was nesting on her head. Sam Wheeler sat next to her, with his hands crossed on his lap. Annie and Ken Shipman sat behind us. John Stone was next to Ken. Mrs. Ham, Debbie, and Jeb were there, too.

The priest said, "We had the privilege of having Donny in our lives. We were made richer for knowing him."

I stood and turned to face the people in the church. The priest stopped talking. Everybody looked at me as though I had words for them, to make sense of this nightmare. I started to speak, but the words wouldn't come out. The words were heavy and weighed me down. I sank to the floor. Then everything went black.

CHAPTER 23

I remembered the church, foggy images of Will, many faces that merged into one, and a white coffin. There were voices. Will's voice was clear, but the others sounded like a poorly-tuned choir. I remembered the hospital, its medicinal smell, and laundry-room cleanliness, but all that was gone. Mrs. Cook's armoire was in the corner of the room, and the air smelled of coffee. I was home.

I couldn't move, or maybe I didn't want to move. I wondered how I was going to get through the rest of my life. Was Donny in pain when he died? It was his heart, so it must have hurt during those last seconds. Did he know he was going to die? Did he think of me?

I pictured Donny in the coffin under the dirt, with his hands crossed and eyes closed. I willed myself to switch places with him. With those thoughts, I transcended from living to surviving.

I tried not to breathe, tried not to think. My body forced me to breathe and I gasped, then I tried not to breathe again. No one had ever loved a son as much as I loved my Donny.

Someone knocked on the door and a moment later, the girls came in carrying a tray.

"Mommy?" said Sissy.

They walked to my bed slowly, leaving the door open. Light from the hallway came into the room. They lay the tray on the nightstand. I saw a sandwich and a pot of coffee.

"You should eat," said Sissy. Claire stood next to her sister.

"Where's Will?" I asked.

"In the barn," said Sissy.

"Leave me alone," I said.

The girls left the room, shutting the door quietly behind them.

Will should be here with me, instead of in that damn barn. He was never around when I needed him. He loved those animals more than he loved me. If he loved me, he would be with me. He had his cows. I had nothing. Damn him and his cows.

The next time I opened my eyes, the door was ajar, and the room was dim with light from the hallway. Someone was standing near the end of the bed.

"Daddy?" I asked.

"He's in the barn. It's me, Claire."

"What's my father doing in the barn?" I asked.

"What?"

"Where's Sissy?"

"In her room."

"How long have you been watching me?"

Claire sat down on the bed. "I miss Donny so much, I don't know what I'm going to do." She folded her hands on her lap and bent her head down.

I had nothing to give. I had no comfort, no energy, and no feelings other than a leaden numbness that made it hard to even blink my eyes. "I can't help you."

Claire started to cry. Her shoulders slumped forward. She wiped her nose with the back of her hand. "You have to help me. You're my mother."

How much did she think I could bear? How could I help Claire when I couldn't even help myself? It would be better if she brought me a razor so I could slit my throat and be done with it.

I pushed her away.

"What are you doing?" Claire's shoulders moved forward as if she was a rag doll.

I pushed harder.

Claire slipped off the bed and landed on the floor with a thud. "Mommy!"

"Leave me alone!" I shouted.

Claire scrambled to her feet and ran out of the room.

A week after the funeral, I went downstairs, and back to the routine of making the coffee, setting the table, and cooking the meals.

I counted on having no thoughts while I worked. I desperately needed no thoughts.

At first, if Claire came into a room and saw me, she'd leave. I didn't have the strength to talk with her, and deal with the tears and words of hurt that were bound to come. I promised myself to make it up to her during one of those unbearably long minutes left in my life. Thank goodness for Sissy. She and Claire were like peanut butter and jelly, like apples and cinnamon. They could help each other get through it.

When the girls went back to school, Claire and I started saying hello and goodbye to each other. At least it was something.

When the girls got home in the afternoon, they sat around the kitchen table, sipped milk, and talked. Eventually, their chatter turned to Donny. They talked about how much they missed him, and I stopped listening. I couldn't bear hearing Donny spoken of in the past. My heart shrank with every word, so I didn't listen to the words. Instead, I listened to the pitch of their voices, high and low interplaying like harmony in a song. I listened to them as I would listen to a bird singing.

Sometimes the girls turned to me, and their voices stopped. They looked at me as if they expected me to say something. I never knew what they were talking about, so I smiled and remained silent. The girls looked at each other, shrugged, and went on talking.

The late afternoon sun cast the cabin's living room in shadows. I turned on the lamp by the sofa.

Angie was staring at the picture over the mantle. "Is that Donny?"

"A long time ago, a neighbor gave Will an aerial photograph of the farm showing the fields, trees, and the roofs of the buildings. I had the photograph enlarged and framed as a gift for Will. It was then that I noticed Donny standing in the driveway, looking up. He couldn't have been five years old. It's one of my favorite things in the house."

"Ma still talks about Donny."

"They were close."

"She shouldn't be mad at you."

"When Donny died, she needed me, and I pushed her away. I couldn't help myself. I was so sad, I didn't know what I was doing."

"One night, I woke up and the light was on. Ma was sitting on my bed. I asked her what was wrong. Ma said she had a surprise. I thought she got a raise. She asked me if I'd like to have a new daddy. She treats me like a child."

"Sometimes mothers do that, even when their children are grown."

"Ma said that Red wanted to get married. She sat there looking at me. I couldn't say congratulations, and I couldn't tell her it was a bad idea, that he didn't deserve her, that she could find someone better. I didn't say anything. She kissed my forehead and left. I want Ma to be happy, but I'm not going to live there if Red moves in."

CHAPTER 24

It had been months since the funeral, and Donny hadn't visited me yet. I expected him to appear at any moment, as Mama and Daddy had appeared to me. My eyes scanned the kitchen constantly, expecting to see Donny in his chair at the table, or leaning against the refrigerator. I walked through the pasture, looking for him. I sat in his room and waited. I asked Daddy where Donny was. He said he didn't know. Maybe Donny got lost and couldn't find his way back. Maybe Donny was visiting Cathleen and Theo. He'd get to me eventually. I was certain of that.

After Donny died, Will talked to me more than at any other time in his life. He talked about the cows, the latest gossip from town, current events, the weather, anything. He talked constantly when we were together.

Eventually, I responded to the health of a cow or an item of news. Will guided me back to the world of the living, one word at a time.

We finally made love. I knew Will was trying to help me and that he loved me. His gentle touch and sweet words told me how much I meant to him. I wanted to cling to Will and stay with him. I wanted to tell him I loved him. But when Will moved on top of me, I floated off to Claire's room. She needed me, too. She was in her bed with her eyes closed. I didn't want to wake her, so I floated into Donny's room and breathed in his scent. The model airplanes he had meticulously put together were still on the bureau. I hovered over them, admiring his work.

When Will shifted off me, I came back. I wanted to hold his head and caress his face, but I had no substance. I wanted to whisper words of comfort, but none came. I left Will lying on the bed and went downstairs. I curled up on Mrs. Cook's red velvet sofa and let the TV lull me to sleep.

Whether there was a crisis in the barn, one of the girls got sick, or dinner burnt into a pile of charcoal, all the days were the same. I cooked, cleaned, and regretted being alive.

Cathleen and Theo dropped by one afternoon. Will and I were at the kitchen table, eating. The girls were at school. Cathleen looked tired.

I got up and put on a fresh pot of coffee.

Will asked her how she was doing. Cathleen said it was hard. I put a bottle of brandy on the table, cleared the dishes, and set out fresh plates for apple pie. I wished Donny was here to see his son.

When Cathleen asked how we were, Will looked at me. "Better," he said.

After I poured the coffee, Cathleen sat Theo down on my lap. He clutched my finger in his little hand and stared up at my face. He had a mole on his left cheek, just like Donny. I touched the mole and he squealed. I put my hand on his belly, and he kicked up his feet. Donny had liked it when I tickled his belly.

Theo's face became blurry. I blinked. My heart started to race. Is the monster's face coming back? I closed my eyes, hoping the sense of panic would pass, and Theo's face would be there when I looked again.

His eyes changed from brown to green. Then the cheeks, which were thin for a baby, swelled and became pink. The hair turned blond. The skin glowed with the freshness of country air. I was light with joy. I knew this baby. I let out a cry and hugged him to my breast.

It was Donny.

I became aware of Will's hand on my arm.

"Let's give Theo back to Cathleen. She has to leave," said Will. I watched him hug his daughter-in-law. "Leave the baby here for an hour sometime soon. It'll do her good."

I reluctantly handed Theo back to his mother. She kissed my cheek, and they left.

"Bye, bye Donny," I said.

Every day when I was alone, I pictured Donny's face. Sometimes I saw him as a young man, and other times as a boy. I talked to the face, saying words aloud so he was sure to hear me.

After a while, I saw him, and he said, "Hi."

I was alive again and happy. I told him I would always be here if he needed me. He smiled, and I smiled, too.

I wondered if I should tell Will I was in touch with our boy. I could just say that Donny was close. If I left it at that, Will wouldn't think I was crazy. He didn't know I talked to Daddy, but this was different, because Will had a right to know about his son. I could say that I heard Donny's voice. No, I would just say he was close. That's all. It would make Will happy. He would ask how Donny was. I would say fine. Then he would kiss me and say I was a good mother.

"I can hear him," I said. We were eating lunch. The girls were at school.

"Hear who?" Will's forearms leaned against the table. He looked up at me as he chewed.

"I mean he's close," I said.

Will stopped chewing. "Who's close?"

"Donny."

Will put his fork down and sat back in his chair. "You've got to stop this, Lil. You hardly say anything, and now you're talkin' to the dead?"

If Will didn't like it, then he didn't have to know anything more about it. "Okay, Will."

After washing the dishes, I went upstairs to rest. I closed the curtains. Light filtered in through the fabric, softening the edges of the objects in the room: the armoire, the coat rack in the corner where I kept Mama's robe, the lamp with fringe on the nightstand, the clock on the table next to the bed. I covered myself with the afghan Belle had knitted for me one Christmas. It had yellow squares trimmed in red and green.

"Are you there, Donny?"

"Yes, Momma," said the little boy.

CHAPTER 25

Will came into the kitchen and handed me a treasure among the mix of bills and fliers that he had collected from the post office in town. He went to Willow Springs every few days to pick up the mail and the local newspaper that came out once a week. The post office considered the farm too remote for mail delivery, so we had to pick it up ourselves. Belle was with him. He often picked her up on the way home, so she could visit for a while and stay for supper. Sissy and Claire were in front of the refrigerator, examining its contents, and whispering to each other.

Will walked in with Belle, handed me the mail, and then left.

I sifted through the letters and noticed one addressed to Lily Phelps and Family.

"What's that?" Belle asked, gesturing to the envelope.

The flap had the letter B printed on it, next to the small picture of a greyhound dog. I picked up a knife and opened the envelope. The paper inside smelled like violets.

"We would welcome your presence at our home," I said, as I read the letter.

"That from Old Lady Bishop?" asked Belle. "She walks around like she has a wad of cotton up her ass."

I read the rest of the invitation to myself.

"She wants us to come to one of her lawn parties," I said.

"I got my invitation last week," said Belle. "Are you sure you want to go, Lily?"

I had waited years for this invitation. I would rub elbows with the elite of Willow Springs. I would eat cake and drink tea from little cups. It was all I could do to stay seated in my chair.

"It's up to you," said Belle. "Sometimes those parties aren't what you expect them to be."

"I'll stay home," said Claire.

"I'll go," said Sissy. "Everybody in town will be there. What should I wear?"

I took the letter upstairs and leaned it against the jewelry box on top of Mrs. Cook's mahogany dresser. I opened the bottom drawer and pulled out the pair of white pants that I had bought for Will years ago. I laid them on the bed carefully and pressed the wrinkles away with my hands.

That night, I waited on the bed for Will to come up.

When he came into the bedroom, he turned to me and asked, "What?"

I pointed my chin toward the pants. Will made a face and picked them up. He took off his jeans and started putting on the white pants. He pulled them up his thighs and then started to wiggle his hips. He inched the pants upwards and soon had them zipped and buttoned.

"How do I look?" Will asked. His face was red.

The pants clung to every muscle.

"Let's see if I can sit down," he said. He walked to the side of the bed keeping his legs stiff. He turned and fell back onto the bed. I bounced when he landed. He looked at me with a puppy dog expression on his face, pleading that I allow him to be free of the misery of the tight pants.

"They don't fit any more, do they?" I said.

The day of the party, Will wore jeans. I picked out a cotton dress with a pattern of purple irises around the hem. I worried that Will was underdressed.

I held Will's arm as we walked up the driveway to Mrs. Bishop's house. The air smelled of freshly cut grass. Tables covered with white tablecloths stood under red and white striped umbrellas. Other tables held trays of sandwiches, bowls of salads, cakes, plates of cookies, and aluminum washbasins with the necks of beer and soda bottles sticking out like porcupine quills. The grand house stood to the side, with its black shutters and enormous slab of granite at the foot of the front door.

Sissy ran past us. "Come on," she shouted. She went to a group of kids who were watching two tall and very skinny boys play badminton, their shirtless chests decorated with red pimples. Boys clustered around one end of the net and girls clustered around the other, in a cornucopia of striped t-shirts and shorts.

Mrs. Bishop would introduce me to everyone, and this party would be the first of many. I would smile graciously and offer my hand. What would I say? I tried to think of what happened in the news recently. I couldn't remember anything.

Mrs. Bishop came up to us, her curly gray hair in perfect disarray, her body thin and her face evenly tan. She had on white sneakers, cut-off jeans, and a t-shirt. I wondered why she hadn't dressed for her party yet. She took our hands and brought us to a table as if she were leading two misbehaving children.

"I'm glad you could come, dear," said Mrs. Bishop, leaning toward me as she spoke. Her granddaughter LuAnn brought me a glass of punch and gave Will a beer.

John Stone came over and sat down. He wore a bright yellow cap advertising a type of calf feed, clean jeans, and a fresh work-shirt. He nodded to me and asked Will if he knew of anyone interested in buying field rock.

Bruce Davis from the Co-Op and his wife Sally headed toward our table. Bruce had put on some weight, and his belly arrived first. Sally was in hot pink shorts and a tight shirt. She held a beer bottle by its neck.

"I'm sorry for your loss," said Sally.

I hadn't thought of Donny for hours, and remembered him now with painful clarity.

John asked Bruce about rock prices. Bruce said he'd be happy to ask around. Then he and Sally left to get some food.

The postmaster approached the table. He was a lanky old man who scattered gossip like a manure spreader in springtime.

"At least Donny wasn't little," said the postmaster. He stayed for a minute. John went with him to get some more beer.

My euphoria evaporated, and in its place came an intense desire to run away. Another couple approached. I couldn't look at them. I didn't want to know who they were. I didn't want to talk to them.

"You still have two children."

I put my hands over my ears and stood. I walked across the lawn and down the driveway carefully, trying not to fall. Everyone would look at me if I fell, and they would laugh. I would be the woman who lost her son and her balance. I got into the truck. A few minutes later, Will and Sissy got in. She slammed the door, and then we drove home.

CHAPTER 26

Each night, I planned topics to discuss with Donny. I chatted with him constantly when we were alone. I was so preoccupied with him that I hardly noticed the increasing height of the girls and the deepening wrinkles on Will's face.

One afternoon, I had my hands in a bowl of ground beef, eggs, and breadcrumbs. I was showing Donny how to make meatloaf. Claire came in.

"Is someone here?" Claire asked. "I thought I heard voices."

I was about to tell Claire to open her mind to the possibility that Donny was in the room.

"What's for supper?" asked Claire.

"Meatloaf. Donny's favorite."

"Donny's dead, Mother."

I kept working the meat mixture with my hands. Maybe one day Claire would see him, but not today. Maybe Donny let me see him because down deep, he loved me more than anyone else. I turned away from Claire and winked at my son.

That Saturday night, young Bobby Wells came to the door. He was tall, very thin, and had perfectly combed hair. Belle was sitting at the table, sipping a cup of tea.

"I'm here to see Claire," Bobby said. He stood by the stove with his hands on his hips. He took a cigarette from his pocket and lit it. "Mind if I smoke?" He blew a puff into the air.

"Guess not." I called up the stairs and in a few minutes, Claire came thundering down the steps.

"Don't wait up," Claire said. She and Bobby were out the door before I could ask them where they were going.

"They left so fast, you'd think the place was on fire," said Belle.

When Will came in, I told him about the Wells boy coming by to pick up Claire. Will said he knew the family. The father drank too much.

"What do you think about Claire dating at sixteen, Mom?" asked Will.

"If she wants to go out with the boys, I suppose you have to let her, 'cause you can't stop 'em," said Belle.

One Saturday night, Claire went out with Bobby. Will went to bed, and I waited up. Claire's eleven o'clock curfew passed, so I moved a chair to the front window, smoked, and let anger build up inside me.

Around midnight, my thoughts went out like daggers to Donny. I asked him why he wasn't taking care of his sister. I worried that Claire had been in an accident. I didn't know if I should call the police. Should I wake Will up? He'd be mad as a hornet. Was she with a boy? She'll get pregnant, and she's not married. Will could force a marriage, but he might kill the boy first.

I asked Donny to go find Claire.

Around two o'clock, a car pulled into the driveway. Claire came into the house and went directly to the refrigerator.

Donny's voice whispered in my ear. "Talk to her, Momma."

"Where have you been?" I asked.

"Out," said Claire.

"Were you having sex?"

"None of your business."

"Tell her she's ruining her life," said Donny.

"You're ruining your life," I said.

"Well, you should know about ruining lives," said Claire.

"Tell her you love her," said Donny.

I brushed my ear with my hand.

"What are you talking about?" I asked.

"You have checked out, Mother. You are gone. You are not here," said Claire. "There's nothing to eat." She slammed the refrigerator door shut.

"Tell her you aren't the enemy. Tell her you love her," said Donny.

"Shut up," I said. I looked right at Donny.

Claire stared at me.

"I'm sorry," I said.

"It's a little late for that." Claire ran up the stairs.

I followed her up, going slowly, like an old woman, clinging to the banister at every step. Will was snoring when I got into bed.

Angie had her eyes on me.

"What is it?" I asked.

"Is Bobby Wells my father?"

"You'll have to ask your mother." All I had were suspicions.

"I've asked her a hundred times. Once, when she was sipping whiskey, she said he was a sweet boy who wasn't ready for marriage, let alone a child. But every month when the bills were due, he was a goddamn-son-of-a-bitch who wouldn't know responsibility if he fell over it. If it's him, I'd like to know."

"What does it say on your birth certificate?"

"Father unknown."

"I'm sorry."

Angie looked down at her hands. "Well, I bet I can tell you something you don't know."

"Shoot."

"One time when Aunt Sissy was over, she and Ma started talking about Donny. Ma sent me off to my room, but I slid out the front and went around the house to the kitchen door so I could hear what they were saying. Ma said she snuck out of her room one afternoon when she was supposed to be doing homework. She went into the barn and helped Grandpa Will with the milking for a while, until he sent her back inside to study."

"If she did her homework half the times we told her to, she'd have done well in school."

"Instead of going into the house, Ma went to the pasture. She walked along her usual path but the ground was wet, and the mud was grabbing at her boots. She went in another direction, to an area that was thick with rocks and junipers. She found a boulder that was wider at the top than at the bottom, making a ledge on one side. It was a strange looking rock, so she peeked underneath. A black and brown fur coat was tucked under the ledge. The fur was mottled and speckled with gray. Ma poked it with a stick, and saw what was left of a snout and teeth. She said she had finally found Benny."

"Claire loved that dog. We all did."

"Then Ma said she got really mad. Benny had left her and so had Donny. There was no one left who really loved her. She said it was your fault. You could have kept Donny alive. You could have made him stay at home and found better doctors. You could have done more."

It was all I could do to keep from bursting into tears.

"Then Aunt Sissy told Ma she was wrong. She said you did everything you could for Donny. He just died. It wasn't anybody's fault. Anyway, Ma said she gathered a pile of loose stones from the field and put them all around Benny, making a little enclosure so no one would ever bother him again. Then she put another rock with mica in it, on top of the boulder. The mica would sparkle in the sunshine, and she'd always be able to find Benny."

"Claire still blames me for Donny's death, doesn't she?" I asked.

"Aunt Sissy told Ma that despite everything that happened, there was always love in that house, and that's what she should remember."

CHAPTER 27

Less than a year after Donny died, Sissy was accepted at the University of Connecticut. She danced around the kitchen reading aloud the letter explaining her acceptance and financial package. Then she stopped abruptly. Belle and I were at the table sipping tea.

"What's the matter?" I asked.

"This isn't enough," said Sissy.

"How much more do you need?" asked Belle.

Sissy told her the amount.

"I'll pay it," said Belle. "You and your sister are going to get everything I own when I die. As far as I'm concerned, the money is yours. I don't give a goddamn how you spend it, so if you want it for your education, that's fine with me."

"I don't believe it! Thank you Grandma Belle." Sissy threw her arms around Belle's neck.

"Just remember one thing. I don't want you getting all mad at your sister when she gets the house and you don't."

Sissy spent the whole summer packing. She filled suitcases and boxes with her things, and stacked them in the back hall, where they waited for the trip, right next to the boots we wore in the barn. She put an old teddy-bear named Marshall on top of the pile.

The morning we drove to school, Sissy got up with Will. She even made breakfast while Claire and I helped in the barn.

We borrowed Belle's car for the trip. The girls sat in the back seat. Sissy chatted the whole way. She talked about getting a job in New

York during the summers. Maybe she'd move there after she graduated. She said she was going to marry money, possibly a doctor.

I had no doubt that Sissy would eventually lead the life she wanted.

We arrived at the school in the commotion of other families piling out of their cars with suitcases full of dreams. We found a place to park near the dorm. Sissy went to the registration office. When she came back, we unloaded the car and carried the packages up to the second floor. Sissy's room had two twin beds, two desks, two closets, two nightstands, and a green floor.

Will's eyes were wet when we said goodbye outside the dormitory of brown stone covered in ivy. I knew he was thinking that he wasn't as smart or accomplished as the kids who surrounded us. He was born to be a farmer. He could tear down an engine, make a sick cow well, and grow corn so tall it became a thing of beauty. It was those kids who weren't as good as him.

One afternoon, Will and I got home late from the grocery store.

"I gotta go as soon as we unload the groceries," he said, plopping two sacks of food down on the counter. He looked out the front windows toward the cows crowding behind the pasture gate. They were waiting for their supper, and for the milking that would bring relief to their swollen udders.

I was stacking cans on the shelf when Claire ambled in.

"See ya later," said Will.

"Dad, can you wait a sec?" asked Claire.

"If I don't get the cows soon, they'll break through the fence," said Will.

"I'm quitting school."

"What?" asked Will. He took off his baseball cap and ran his fingers through his hair. "How are you going to support yourself?"

"I'll get a job."

"Where are you going to live?"

"I'll find a place."

"Who's going to hire you?"

Claire's face turned red. "Anything's better than staying here."

"Number one, you're only sixteen. Two, you aren't quitting school. And three, we'll talk about this when I come in from the barn." The door slammed behind him as he left the room.

When Will finished chores, it was long after dark. He came inside and said, "Where's Claire?"

"Gone," I said.

"Why'd you let her go?"

"You're never here. You spend all your time in the barn, or out in those damn fields."

"It takes me longer to do things now, Lil. I don't go as fast as when I was younger. What do you expect me to do? I've got to take care of the animals. I've got to keep going."

"I couldn't stop her. A car pulled up to the house and then she ran downstairs with her suitcase. She went right out the door. Didn't even say goodbye."

"Why didn't you come get me?"

"You were milking."

Will limped across the floor to the hallway. He climbed the stairs heavily, one thump at a time. He always limped now.

I couldn't stand being alone in the kitchen. It was as though the air was full of daggers looking for a target. I fixed four white bread sandwiches, with ham slices and tomato, and made a pot of fresh coffee. I put it all on a tray and brought it upstairs for Will. He couldn't go to bed without his supper.

Belle came over the next morning. She told us that Claire had phoned and said she was living with friends in town. When she found her own place, she'd let us know. Belle said she sounded okay, and handed Will a piece of paper with a phone number on it for emergencies.

A few weeks later, the phone rang and an operator asked if we'd accept a collect call from Nevada. Will and I held the receiver between us, so we both could hear.

"I got married," said Claire.

"Do we know him?" I asked.

"That doesn't matter, Mother. I'm happy, and you should be, too."

"You get the hell home, young lady!" Will's voice stormed through the kitchen. The phone went silent.

"Are you there?" asked Will.

"Yes, Dad."

"I want you to get home where you belong. If you need money, I'll send you some. Just come home."

"Dad, please. I'm a married woman."

"What have you done?" I cried.

Claire hung up.

She called again later that night and said she lived in a big house, had a fast car, many friends, and went to fancy parties.

Claire offered no specifics and no address, but she gave us a phone number. Her husband's name was Frank, and everyone called him Frankie.

"What does he do for a living?" I asked.

"You don't need to know what he does Mother, he just does. He's a player."

"What's that?" I asked.

"I have to go."

We drove to Belle's house to tell her that Claire was married.

We said we knew nothing about the man. Frankie was a player, whatever that meant. We didn't mention the house or the parties, for it was all too new and too hard to understand.

I said that Claire sounded happy.

"Hurts that she didn't tell us before she got married," said Belle.

"Ma was married?" asked Angie. "She never told me that."

"After Claire left Frankie and Nevada, she came over, and I asked her why she had left her husband. She said they never got married. It was a lie. Claire knocked the wind out of me just as if she had hit me in the chest with a bat."

"But is Frankie my father?"

"I don't know."

"Why don't you know? You're her mother!"

"When she came back to Willow Springs, she found a place to live, and got a job. She started seeing Bobby Wells almost right away. Then she told us she was pregnant. I suppose it could have been Frankie or Bobby. She wouldn't tell me. She wanted you, Angie. She always worked hard to provide for you. You have to know that."

"She never told me anything."

"Maybe she's not the only one to blame. There were things I never said to her that every mother should say to her daughter. I never told Claire about sex, or what to look for in a man. I never told her how important family was, and to be happy with herself. I was more comfortable with the calves in the barn than I was talking to my own daughter."

"I don't know why she's so secretive about my father. She knew her father. I don't see why she won't tell me about mine."

"Maybe she's embarrassed."

"Ma doesn't get embarrassed."

"Maybe she didn't want to share you."

"That's ridiculous. Besides, she wants to marry Red. I would rather slit my wrists than call him Daddy."

"Don't talk like that."

"It's true."

"I don't know why Claire does half the things she does. I don't know why she started dating Red in the first place."

"She always said pickings were slim in this neck of the woods."

"That's what Will used to say."

CHAPTER 28

One night, through the haze of sleep, I saw Donny in the kitchen, in the black suit he had worn to his funeral. His image was so vivid I thought this couldn't be a dream. As Will snored next to me, Donny sat in his chair, the one to the left of Will's at the head of the table. Daddy was there too, sitting in Will's chair. Will didn't like anyone sitting in his chair. I'd have to ask Daddy to move. Daddy held a spoon in his right hand and a cigarette in his left. I saw myself at the stove in jeans and one of Will's shirts. I was cooking oatmeal. I went to the table with the pot and scooped a big serving onto Donny's plate.

He looked down at the food. Then he looked up at me with sunken eyes. His skin was drawn tight over his bones.

"I can't eat nothin' Momma, 'cause I'm dead." Donny tilted his head back and laughed. His mouth was open so wide, I could see his back teeth. He laughed as though he had heard the funniest joke in the world. Then he pointed a bony finger at me, and laughed harder. Daddy laughed too, until he coughed and gagged. I poured him a glass of water.

"No Donny, no," I said. "Don't laugh at me. Why are you laughing at me?" I loved Donny so dearly, and he was laughing at me for feeding him. He was being mean, making fun of me.

Then I was awake. Donny and Daddy were gone. I was in bed, and Will was next to me. I made out the shape of Mrs. Cook's armoire and the lamp with the fringe on the table next to me. I settled back onto the pillow. The dead, whom I had loved so faithfully, were

181

mocking me. Why hadn't Daddy kept Donny alive, and why hadn't Donny helped Claire? The dead were lazy. The dead were useless. I was angry with the dead. When Will's alarm clock rang, I didn't tell him that Donny had laughed at me in my dreams.

I put on Mama's fuzzy slippers and her terrycloth robe, and went out into the hallway, only to see the closed doors of my children's rooms. One was dead, and the two who lived were gone. I went back to my room and cried.

That night at supper, I told Will I couldn't stay in the house any longer. I couldn't pass by their empty bedrooms every day.

"You're gonna miss them no matter where you go," said Will.

"I know, but I think it would be easier if we moved someplace else. Started over."

"Lily, don't you think it's a little late to start over?"

"You don't understand, Will. I really need to move." I braced myself for a fight.

"Okay." Will took another bite of his food.

"What?"

"I wouldn't mind retiring."

I didn't think Will would ever want to leave the farm. "Are you kidding?"

"Why would I kid about retiring?"

We started making plans that night, building to an excitement that spilled onto the bed, where we made love.

That night, I told Will to touch my back and stroke my neck. I kissed his ears and the nipples on his chest. I took his weight. I told him when to go faster and when to slow down to make it last. I was there for every second. I smelled his scent and felt drips of his sweat trickle down my neck. When he moaned, I moaned too.

Afterward, lying next to him, I realized I had just made love for the very first time in my life. This old farmer had linked his soul to mine. We had made it through good and bad times together. I loved him more now than ever. I didn't want to jump up and dance a jig. I just wanted to stay right where I was.

We snuggled under the sheets, giggling like two children. We decided how much we should get from the sale. Will said he didn't care if the buyer carved up the land and sold it to a developer. He didn't care if the place fell down a goddamn hole. He talked about money and working less. The most important thing was finding a good home for the herd. We fell asleep in each other's arms.

We decided to build a cabin in the woods. If we had to, we could stay with Belle for a while. At the equipment auction, we would sell Mrs. Cook's furniture and even the pots and pans, to make some extra money. When I thought about it though, I realized I didn't want to get rid of the dark, heavy furniture, for it reminded me of the times when we were all together.

Selling the land was straightforward, but when it came to the cows, Will wanted things done a certain way. He wanted to keep the herd together. He wanted the cows to be in a clean barn. He wanted them to go to a solid operation, where the owner wouldn't sell them little by little to pay off debt. He wanted someone who would be kind to the animals and take good care of them.

After months of showing the place, we finally had an offer on the land, contingent on Will selling the herd. Soon, he got an offer from a farmer in New Hampshire. It was for a good price, and the cows would go to a well-established farm. The last phone conversation we had with the new owner was about the date and time the cattle trucks would arrive.

I went into the barn with Will that last morning. The animals knew something was different. Will got them up earlier than usual. He had to poke some of them with a stick to get them going. A few came into the barn right away, because they always did. The ones that were lying down stood with great effort, moving their heads forward while summoning power in their massive shoulders and hips to lunge their bodies forward and upwards to a standing position. They made their way into the barn calmly, slowly, taking the time to pause and flick their tail at a fly, or scrutinize the door before going inside.

Will clicked each stanchion shut and gave each cow extra grain to get rid of it. He was quiet that morning. There was no banter about the weather or politics. After so many years together, the big, lumbering beasts were Will's friends, co-workers, and confidants.

On that last morning together, it was hard to talk.

After he milked each cow, he put his hand on her back for a moment, the touch of human flesh to cowhide, warm to warm, soul to soul. Some animals turned their heads and looked at him as he touched them with his big, calloused hand. Will could laugh at a joke, scowl at evil, and cry when words were not enough, but his hands told the story of his life. The fingers could squeeze the tender teat of a cow, crush a beer can, hold a pen, and turn the delicate pages of a book, even though Will hadn't read a book in a long time.

Who knew if there was anything more to those black and white creatures than their memory of Will's kindness in feeding and caring for them? His touch that morning, like any morning, was just a touch. The animals were quiet, too. They knew something was different.

The farm up in New Hampshire, where the herd was going, was milking a hundred head already. Will's girls were their next expansion. The new owner had invited us to drop by anytime. It would never be the same though, like a child who grew up and left home. Love was there, but hidden behind other things like new friends, new adventures, and new ambitions. With cows, love went to the new hands that fed them. Maybe the cows would remember Will, but eventually they would look to their new owners for food, water, and the drizzle of affection they might get.

Two cattle trucks arrived just as we were finishing chores. The first truck backed into the barnyard through the open gate. The driver lowered the ramp to the ground. It looked like a big brown tongue hanging out of the back of the truck. Some cows walked up the ramp willingly, after a prod or two with a stick. Some followed a pail of grain into the truck, but that caused commotion inside among the cows who felt they had been cheated out of their fair share. Others had to be pulled into the truck with a rope.

Except for when Donny died, I think this was the saddest day of Will's life.

The trucks left for the drive north well before noon, and then Will disappeared.

I found him sitting on a bale of hay in the barn, his elbows on his knees, looking down at his feet. The barn had never been so quiet. Hooves weren't shuffling along the floor. Bovine cries weren't telling Will to hurry up with the feeding and the milking. There was the sense already that the barn had been empty for a long time.

I had a bottle of champagne and two glasses with me. I sat down next to Will, and we toasted each cow: Cupcake, Mildred, Bessie, and the others. By the time we finished the champagne, our arms were around each other, and we were missing the cows together.

Within three months, we had moved in with Belle, and were building our cabin in the woods. We had kept a twenty-acre parcel of the pasture's woodland that was next to the road, with a natural clearing in the middle. Will cut down trees, moved boulders, and built a road to the clearing. Nothing went to waste. He made a kitchen counter from one of the trees, and cut the rest for firewood. He moved the rocks to a pile on the edge of the clearing and arranged some like a table and chairs. He used other rocks to create a place for Theo to play. He made a long stone wall leading to the house. By the time the cabin kit arrived, we could drive to the site, sit on our rock furniture drinking coffee, and imagine what it would be like living there.

The cabin kit included logs, rafters, decking, roofing material, tresses, flooring, insulation board, support beams, and everything else needed to build the structure. We hired two carpenters from town, John Marchetti and his son, because they had put up a cabin once before. The father and son were both named John, so the father went by the name Old John. The son went by the name Little John, even though he was twice the size of his father. Little John presented a strangely graceful sight in overalls, dancing on the edge of the roof.

We went to the work site every day. Will helped by carrying away debris, fetching tools, and most importantly, knowing when to stay out of the way. I usually brought coffee and doughnuts in the morning. Little John waited until everyone else had their fill of doughnuts and then finished them off, no matter how many were left.

I sat in the pickup truck while Will worked, and watched my new house emerge from the dirt, growing up as if it were a strange sort of tree. Sometimes Cathleen and Theo came by and sat with me in the truck. Theo had just started to walk, and got restless easily, so the visits were brief. I longed for more time with Theo, so I could feel like a mother was supposed to feel. I wanted to remember what that was like.

The cabin wouldn't be the big house I had dreamed of when I was young. It wouldn't be fancy in any way. The cabin was the result of a new dream that belonged to Will and me. This dream took into account how we wanted to live: peacefully, simply, and quietly. It wasn't a house that would inspire Mrs. Bishop to include us in her social circle. It was a place where we could wake up to the music of birds, and hear an acorn drop to the ground. As I watched my cabin take shape, I hoped that the worst experiences of my life were behind me.

Finally, the cabin was finished. It looked like it belonged where it was. The honey-colored logs complemented the woods like a diamond broach pinned to a black dress. There was no lawn. Once the construction was over and Will had raked the dirt around the house, the land seemed to become part of the woods again. The pine needles, pinecones, leaves, and sticks stayed where they fell, making it look like the cabin had always been there, and that the woods had not been disturbed in its creation.

The main room inside was large and open, with a kitchen along one wall, separated from the rest of the room by the counter Will had made. A fireplace stood on the opposite side, its smooth gray stones stretching all the way up to the ceiling. The aerial shot of the farm, with Donny waving from the driveway, was over the mantle. A hallway in the back of the house led to the bedrooms and a bath.

I put Mrs. Cook's red velvet sofa in front of the fireplace. Along one wall, I put the old bookcase with the grapevine carving that we had carried to the milking parlor that winter long ago, when the snow wouldn't stop falling. Mrs. Cook's dining room table and the chairs with red tapestry on the seats dominated the middle of the room.

I added a few new rugs, fresh curtains in the kitchen, and a big bowl of fruit on the dining room table. I found it felt more like home when a little of the old was mixed in with the new.

"I miss Great Grandma Belle," said Angie.

"I'm glad you got to know her."

"It was nice that Grandma Belle left the house to Ma."

"It was all arranged when Sissy went off to college. Belle's money went to Sissy because she needed it for tuition. Claire got the house. When you were born, your mother was living in a small apartment above the drug store, so Belle invited Claire to move in with her. It was good for all of you. Belle made it to one-hundred-and-five years, and I think you and your mother had something to do with that."

"What do you mean?"

"You brought her joy and made her want to live."

CHAPTER 29

I was sneaking a cigarette in my new kitchen and talking to Daddy, when I heard a noise. I stubbed out the cigarette and waved my hands to get rid of the smoke. Then I shooed Daddy away. Cathleen came in with little Theo toddling behind her.

Cathleen kissed my cheek. "Would you watch Theo for a few hours?"

It felt like I had won the lottery.

Cathleen put down a diaper bag that was brimming with toys, kissed my cheek again, and left. I watched her car go down the driveway and along the road, until I couldn't see it any more.

Finally, I was alone with little Theo. We were in my new house where nothing bad had ever happened. I would be a grandmother playing with her grandson, without guilt, without strangeness, and without fear. It would just be Theo and me, but the memory of Donny was so vivid, it was like he was in the room. He wasn't, though. He hadn't come to the new house. I wondered if he ever would.

Theo waddled to the bag Cathleen had left and pulled out a yellow dump truck. He showed me the big black wheels. He pulled out Mr. Collins, a teddy-bear with blue button eyes, and said I could hold him if I wanted. He said Mr. Collins was good to sleep with because he was so soft, it was like sleeping with your mommy.

When Theo climbed onto my lap, I noticed the unmistakable scent of a baby in need of a diaper change. I put Theo down on the table and took his clothes off slowly, piece by piece, putting them to the side. Then I opened the diaper, lifted his legs at the ankles, and wiped away the mess under him. I put a clean diaper in place of the dirty one. With a fresh cloth, I cleaned inside the folds and crevices. I put my hand on Theo's belly, and he giggled. He was pink and beautiful. He took hold of my finger. As I gazed down at the cherub face, the raspy voice from my nightmares called my name.

Suddenly I was in the old house, in the kitchen with the dancing spoons on the walls. It hurt between my legs. Something wet trickled all the way down to my knees. The man sighed and leaned back in the chair. Then he grabbed me by the arm pulled me right up to his face. He fished in his pocket and pulled out a knife.

He opened the knife and pressed the blade against my throat. I thought I was going to die. Terrified, I stared at the dancing spoons and held my breath.

"You need to be a good girl, and do what I say." His breath smelled bad. "You don't tell anyone a thing about this. You're going to be a good girl, or else I'm going to find you. And I'm going to slit your doll's throat, and then your mama's throat, and your daddy's throat, and it will be your fault, because you weren't a good girl." He sneered. "You hear me? Everywhere you go, everything you do, I'll be watching. You be a good girl from now on, and do what I say, or that's gonna be it for your mama and daddy and your doll. You can put that in the bank."

I wanted to say he didn't have to kill Mama, because she was sick already, but I was too scared. He put the knife down and let go of my arm.

I grabbed Liza my doll, my dress, and my panties, and ran outside. I went behind the shed, where I had a good view of the front door. It hurt down there between my legs, and I cried as I got dressed. It was cold. Blood trickled down the inside of my legs. I put my panties on anyway. The man had killed me already, and I was bleeding to death. Daddy would find me dead behind the shed. I squeezed Liza. Please don't let me die, Liza.

The man came out on the porch, and looked from side to side.

"You remember what I said," he shouted. Then he went back into the house.

Liza and I climbed the cherry tree in the back yard and hid in the branches. It hurt to climb the tree, but I had to, so I wouldn't die. Nobody ever died in a cherry tree.

I heard Daddy's car before I could see it, because it was so quiet outside you could hear an engine from way off. I climbed down the tree and hid behind the shed. I was never so glad to see Daddy, but I stayed hidden, because the man might come out and hurt me again. Then Daddy would have to kill him. Daddy went into the house. A little bit later, the man came out carrying the sawhorses. He went into the house again and came out with the rest of his things, loading everything onto the back of his truck. On his last trip, he dropped crumpled pieces of wallpaper into the trashcan. When he left, I ran inside.

I was going to tell Daddy that the man had taken my clothes off and had hurt me until pudding came out and there was blood and I was going to die. I found Daddy in the kitchen looking at the new wallpaper. He seemed so sad that I didn't dare say anything. He said Mama wasn't coming home.

That night, I tiptoed outside and threw my bloody panties in the trash, carefully tucking them under pieces of discarded wallpaper so Daddy wouldn't see them.

The face with crooked lips and pinhead eyes looked up at me from my dining room table. It was starting all over again. I was terrified just like when I was a little girl. I could barely breathe.

"Get out of here you bastard," I said, staring down at the face. I was so scared I could barely hear myself. I wanted to run.

"But it's just Theo." *Donny's voice.*

He looked sad. So did Mama, standing next to him.

"Mama?" I said. "Why are you crying? Where's Daddy?"

"It's the man. Ken Shipman's daddy. Don't you see him?" I pointed a shaking finger at the table.

"It's Theo," said Donny. "He wouldn't hurt you."

"No, he wouldn't." I felt tears on my cheeks. "It was Ken Shipman's daddy all those times I screamed at you and ran away, leaving you all alone. I didn't want to, but I couldn't help it. I wanted to be a good mother, but I couldn't bear to look at you. *He* was rattling around in my head all those years, coming out. Doing damage."

"I didn't think you loved me," said Donny.

"I loved you more than my own life, and I still do."

A tear trickled down Donny's cheek.

I had to get past the fear for Theo's sake and for Donny's. I summoned my will and gazed down at the pinhead eyes and the sneer. I forced myself to remember everything I didn't want to remember—everything that had come to me in bits and pieces over the years. I pieced together what had happened during each second, remembering every word, the hundreds of details, all of it.

"Get the hell out of here you son-of-a-bitch," I yelled. I summoned all my strength and shook my fists at the figure on the table. As Theo screamed, I willed Ken Shipman's daddy to leave and never come back—to finally be dead and buried. Gradually, the sneer and pinhead eyes faded from Theo's face. By the time I could see Theo's red, tear-stained cheeks, it felt like a fresh wind had blown through the house taking the bad away. Relief washed over me, leaving me almost too tired to stand.

I clutched the side of the table. "He's gone. Don't you see?"

Donny and Mama were fading away, too.

"I want you to know what happened to me when I was a little girl. Donny, don't go! Mama!" I called. "Where are you going? Please don't go. Let me tell you."

Then I noticed Will standing in the doorway, staring at me with wide eyes. He opened his mouth as if he was going to say something, but he didn't. He came over and quickly dressed Theo. As he went to the door carrying the child, I must have passed out. The next thing I knew, it was night and I was in my bed.

Will was sitting next to me. I wanted to tell him everything, but I was too tired. He told me I was going away for a while to a place where I could get some help.

I paused to catch my breath. Then Angie spoke.

"Yesterday, when I got home from school, I started cooking like I do every afternoon. Then Red came in. He must have parked on the street, 'cause I didn't see his truck pull into the driveway. He kind of snuck in and caught me by surprise. I didn't have time to run off."

I braced myself.

"Red got a beer out of the fridge and sat there looking at me. It made me feel creepy. I tried to finish up fast so I could get out of there. Then he said it was about time I knew what it was to be a woman. I told him if he didn't leave me alone, I was going to tell Ma. He said I could tell her what I wanted, 'cause she wasn't going to believe me. She was too much in love with him."

"What happened, Angie?"

My granddaughter looked past me, toward the windows. She was wringing her hands.

"He grabbed me and started kissing me. I tried to get away, but it was like I was in a vise. I grabbed the fry pan from the stove and hit him in the head, but the angle was funny and I think I just burned him. He stumbled backwards and grabbed his head. Burgers were all over the floor. He stood there for a minute, looking surprised. Then he started swearing. I just froze. He undid his belt buckle and said, 'I'll teach you something, alright.' I turned to run just as Ma came in through the door. She said what the hell is going on. Red said I pounced on him like a wildcat. Ma asked me if that was true, and I said yeah, I hit him because he was coming after me. Red called me a damn liar. He said I needed a good thrashing and he was ready to do it. Ma told him that if I needed a thrashing, she'd take care of it herself. She told me to go to my room. Red had a smirk on his face. I ran upstairs and locked my door. A little while later, they both left. I was awake when they both came back in the middle of the night. They went right into Ma's room, and I came here first thing in the morning."

"You're not going back there."

"After I hit Red, I wished he was dead."

"I'll finish that job if I have to."

Angie put her arms around me. I took her by the hand into the kitchen. I put her to work peeling carrots and potatoes, while I seared the stew meat—anything to keep us busy and away from our thoughts. When the ingredients were in the pot, I turned the heat down and poured some brandy into tumblers.

"This will settle your nerves," I said, as I handed her a glass. "I'll go over to Claire's house tomorrow and get your things. You don't have to come with me, unless you want to."

"Okay, Grandma."

CHAPTER 30

Angie ate the stew with her head bent forward, her raven hair hiding part of her face. Except for the hair color, I could have been looking at a younger version of myself.

I told Angie how Will had shipped me up to Homestead House in New Hampshire after he caught me shaking my fists at Theo like a madwoman and calling for Donny. Homestead House was a place for people with issues like depression and whatnot. Will told me I had to go, and that he'd been worried about me for a while. So I went. Thank goodness Daddy went with me, because otherwise, I would have gone crazy.

I told the doctors about Ken Shipman's daddy. They said I had repressed the memory, and it had come out in little explosions, bit by bit. The doctors helped me put it all together, made me see what Ken Shipman's daddy had done to me, and how my behavior had affected how I'd treated Donny. They said that years of not remembering ate me up like a cancer. I believed it. I didn't talk about seeing Daddy or Donny after they died. I figured it wasn't any of their business.

I knew what I had done was wrong, even when I was doing it. When that raspy voice boomed in my head, I did anything to avoid it, including screaming and running away from my son. I had tried to be a good mother.

It was funny how a few minutes in a life can change its course.

At Homestead House, I had to sit in a circle with other people, and we had to talk about what was bothering us. I said I missed my husband and my family. I told them about Donny's death. I talked about Claire and how I couldn't help her cope with her brother dying. I listened to people moan in the dayroom. I had to get used to another smell that was like a mixture of ammonia, baby powder, and piss. It was like my first days at the Co-Op, getting used to smells I didn't like. Thank goodness Daddy was with me.

Before I left Homestead House, the doctors said I had to forgive myself, because that was all I could do.

The girls were there when Will and I pulled into the driveway. Sissy had driven home from college just for my homecoming. I told her she looked tired. She had to stay up late to finish some work, and didn't get to the cabin until two o'clock that morning. Claire was back from Nevada by then. She said she always knew I was nuts. It hurt when she said that, but I guess I deserved it. Sissy put one of Annie Shipman's casseroles in the oven for supper. It was ground beef and macaroni, with cheese on top. We sat in our chairs around the dining room table in the new cabin. It didn't feel like home yet. Sissy spooned the food onto our plates.

"Did they treat you good?" asked Will.

I said the people there were very nice, but I didn't like being around crazies all the time.

"Did you talk about us?" asked Sissy.

"She's not supposed to say what she told the doctors," said Will.

"That's okay, Will. I told them how I had been abused as a little girl and how that made me treat Donny." Sissy nodded. I was glad Will had explained things to her and Claire. "I had a lot of trouble dealing with Donny's death, and wasn't able to help you girls, even though you needed me."

Claire looked down at her food.

"I hope you forgive me," I said.

"Of course we forgive you, Lil," said Will.

I put my fork down. "I wish I could ask Donny to forgive me."

"You were his mother. He had to forgive you," said Sissy.

I smiled. He had to love me. He had no choice. "I smoke, you know."

"You've always smoked," said Sissy.

"I don't know why you tried to hide it. You think we couldn't smell the cigarette smoke on you? Don't be ridiculous," said Claire.

"Why didn't you say something?" I asked.

"Because you didn't want us to know," said Will.

After I got home, I searched the cabin for Donny, but didn't find him. Then I drove to the farm thinking Donny might be there. The new owners would never let me search the house, even if I told them I had left something behind. Maybe he was in the pasture. He loved the pasture. I could start there. I asked the new owners if I could walk along the cow paths. They said to help myself.

It was strange opening the gate and stepping onto the tufted grass, knowing I was on somebody else's land. As I took that first step, I realized Donny would never be sick again. Instead of letting my past kill me little by little, I had faced it and had survived. Days of possibility lay ahead.

The grass was tall, for there were no cows to keep it trimmed. The new owners were going to clear away the rocks and plant Christmas trees. Good luck to them, I thought.

I wandered along the leftmost path and came upon a large rock that was wide at the top and narrow at the bottom. A piece of mica rested on the stone, and there was a wall of smaller rocks against one side. I thought of Benny, and could almost hear his bark. Then his soft fur brushed against my leg as he ran by. He dashed to the gate and stood there, his tail wagging. A man stood at the gate, waving. I thought it was the new owner, but then I recognized Ed's overalls and pipe. He winked at me. On the breeze came the voices of twelve little calves calling for their supper.

I walked all the way to the valley that stretched like a lazy cat down to the stream. I followed the stream out to the old sawmill. I didn't want to go home, but then again, I already was home.

I didn't find Donny. I figured he was home with Cathleen and Theo where he belonged. I was okay with that.

When I got to the cabin, it was almost dark. Will said it was good that I was taking long walks to keep myself fit.

I never looked for Donny again.

Cathleen brought Theo over the week I got home, but never left me alone with him again. I don't know if Will told her everything that had happened, but I suspect he told her enough.

Will said that Ken and Annie Shipman had come over frequently while I was gone. Annie brought over food for supper a couple of times a week. John Stone came by too, asking how I was getting on.

Will wanted me to have John, Ken and Annie over for supper, to thank them for helping out and to celebrate my coming home. It was a cool fall day, and I made a roast with carrots and potatoes. There was plenty of cold beer, and the girls made cookies. Belle came over, too. After we ate, the girls took a walk. John and Will talked about the price of milk. Belle took Annie aside to show her the sweater she was knitting. Ken and I grabbed a few beers and went outside for a cigarette. I didn't hide my smoking any more. I had learned that secrets could hurt people, and stilt lives.

Ken's hair had turned white, and age had brought out his father's features. I shivered as I looked at him, remembering the agony his father had caused me. But it was his father who had hurt me, not Ken. It was hard to remember that when I looked at Ken's face.

We sat on the boulders near the side of the house.

"Something happened to me when I was little. I think you need to know about it. Even if you don't, I need to say it," I said. Ken's nose was swollen from drinking, and he had his father's crooked lips.

"I was in grade school. Your father came over to work on the kitchen. He was putting up wallpaper with dancing spoons; the same paper you have in your front hall."

"It was left over from a job," said Ken.

"The job was my old kitchen. The day he put it up, my daddy was at the hospital because Mama was sick. I was all alone."

"Oh, no."

"Your father raped me." I took a tissue from my pocket and blew my nose. "I know it was him because when Annie and I were cleaning out his things, I found the shoes he wore that day. I'll never forget those shoes."

Ken covered his face with his hands.

"I'm not trying to hurt you, but I need to talk about this."

"I knew," said Ken.

"What?"

"I didn't know about you, but I knew what he was doing. When I was thirteen, he got a job over in Four Rivers. One night, a man came to the house and told my father that if he ever saw him again, he was going to kill him. Then he said to leave his little girl alone. He beat my father bloody. I ran out and told the man to stop, and he left. Everything made sense after that. Dad always took jobs away from home, except occasionally, when he couldn't find anything else.

Mother never wanted me to be around him, but I don't think she knew exactly what he was up to until that night. I didn't know either. He moved to Florida after that, and it was good riddance as far as I was concerned. I always thought it was a blessing that he didn't work in town much. If he had, I wouldn't have been able to live here. I became a police officer so I could do something about scum like him. Even at the end, he asked me why I hated him, as if it was all still a secret. I said it was because he was a sick son-of-a-bitch, and he just looked at me like he didn't know what I was talking about."

"People are scared of the dead, but it's the living that you really have to watch out for," I said.

"Annie wanted kids, but I said no. I couldn't run the risk of having a child who might grow up to be like him." Ken brought his beer can to his forehead as if he was cooling a fever. "I'm so sorry, Lily."

"Does Annie know?" I asked.

The cabin door banged shut and Annie came down the steps. "Time to go, Ken."

Ken stood. "We'll see you later, Lily. Thanks for having us over."

I let him go without saying anything more. I figured Ken didn't need to know the rest of the story.

CHAPTER 31

"There's one more thing," said Angie. "You haven't told me how Grandpa Will died."

"I don't want to talk about it. It makes me sad."

"You're already sad."

Will wasn't feeling good all day. Then at supper, he picked at his food and asked me to wrap it up for tomorrow. I should have known something was wrong, because he never skipped a meal. I should have called the doctor right away, but I didn't. I thought it was a sour stomach or maybe the flu. I gave him some aspirin and told him to go to bed. It was a warm night. I had the windows open in the bedroom. The air was moist. When I got into bed, Will was asleep.

He moaned in the middle of the night and woke me up.

"What is it?" I reached over and touched him.

"I didn't want to wake you."

"What's wrong?"

"I don't feel good."

"Your stomach?" I turned on the light. Will was pale and barely breathing. "I'm calling the paramedics."

He grabbed my wrist. "I love you, Lil."

"I love you too, Will."

He didn't let go.

I put my hand over his. "I'll be right back."

Will's eyes closed, and he shuddered. Then he sighed and relaxed its grip. I ran to the phone and dialed the emergency number.

"It's Lily Phelps. My husband needs help!"

I opened the front door and turned on the lights. Then I went back to Will and sat next to the bed. Every time I tried to focus my eyes, tears fell to my cheeks.

The Rescue Squad arrived quickly, and two men carrying packs ran into my bedroom. One of them told me to wait in the living room for the ambulance.

Ken Shipman walked in.

"Are you always on duty?" I asked.

"Make me a cup of coffee, Lil," he said.

"I got to wait for the ambulance."

"I'll take care of it."

I went into the kitchen and made the coffee. Ken went into the bedroom and came back a few minutes later.

"Is he going to be alright, Ken?"

"You got anything to eat?"

I was making a sandwich when the ambulance arrived. Two more men came in with a gurney, like the one they had used to take Daddy away.

When Ken was finishing his sandwich, they carried Will through the living room with a sheet pulled over his face.

"So that's that," I said.

Ken got up slowly and closed the front door. "What's Claire's number?"

"Let her sleep. She'll know soon enough."

"You can't stay here alone."

"I'm going to be alone a lot from now on. I may as well get used to it."

Ken put his hand on my shoulder. "I'd stay if I could, but I really got to go."

"So go."

When Ken left, I turned the lights off and wrapped myself in a blanket. I sat on the sofa, peering into the far corners of the room. "Will, are you there?" Life had stopped again. There was nothing left to do, but wait for Will.

Angie put her hand on mine, as we sat at the table with the remains of the meal in front of us. Then light flashed through the window. It was Red's truck.

I ran to the closet and pulled out Will's shotgun. I had time to load a single shell before the door swung open. Claire came in first. She had the look of a wild woman. Red came in next and stood beside her. I pointed the gun at his chest.

"What did you do to my car?" Claire shouted.

I cocked the hammer. Angie whimpered.

"Never mind the car," I said.

Claire turned to me and the gun. "Put that thing down!"

"Not so long as Red's here," I said.

"Then you'll have to shoot me first." Claire stepped in front of Red.

I glanced at Angie. Her eyes were as big as balloons.

"Don't shoot Ma." Angie grasped my arm.

I nodded, and then stepped to the side so I could still get Red if I had to.

"You could have killed Red when you hit him on the hed with the fry pan." Claire's eyes looked like the inside of her head was on fire.

"He was coming after me," said Angie. She hiccupped through a sob.

Claire turned to Red. "Were you?"

"I already told you what happened. And she's a damned liar," said Red pointing a finger at Angie.

Claire didn't move.

"Tell your crazy son-of-a-bitch mother to put that gun down," said Red.

"That ain't going to happen," I said.

"Were you going after Angie?" asked Claire.

"Of course not," said Red gazing down at the floor.

Claire turned from Angie to Red, as if she was trying to figure out who to believe.

"All I ever wanted was a family," said Claire. "You're the first man who ever wanted a family with me."

"I know, baby. Once I find a job, we can get married, like we talked about today," said Red. "All I need is a job. You could call your nephew, Theo, and put in a good word for me, get me hired back at the yard."

I spoke up. "Angie and I are your family. Don't you know that? Ask him why he got fired from the lumberyard."

"The men there don't like him and made him look bad in front of the boss," said Claire.

"My ass," I said.

"What do you know, old woman?" Red sneered at me.

"You call me old woman again, and I'm going to shoot you just for fun."

"You don't know nothin'."

"I know what Ken Shipman told me."

"He don't know nothin'."

"He knows you were at the Snake Pit with that secretary from the office, and you were kissing her. I bet you're screwing her, too."

"You don't know what you're talking about." Red glanced at the floor again.

Claire was staring at Red. The fire was gone from her eyes. For a moment, we were all still, like figures in a painting. Then Claire spoke softly. "You better go."

"But I love you," said Red.

Claire stepped away from the door. "Just go."

Red wiped his eyes and pointed his finger at me. "This ain't over, old woman."

"Maybe not," I said. "But if you show up here again, I guarantee you'll be dead before I am."

Red gave me a look that would peel paint. Then he left. I moved to the door, the shotgun still in my hands, and watched him drive off. Angie and Claire stood behind me. When the woods returned to complete darkness, I realized things had become as normal as they would get for a while.

I turned to face the girls. In the shadows of the hallway that led to the bedroom I had shared with Will, there stood a man. He had silver hair and a smile that I knew better than my own heart.

"They come back when they're needed, don't they Angie?" I asked, pointing toward the hallway.

Angie smiled, and slipped her hand in mine. "I guess they do."

Claire turned her head toward the hallway. "What are you two looking at?"

THE END

AFTERWORD

The setting for *Purple Trees* is rural New England in the 1960s through the 1980s. Families put money into modernizing their barns according to new standards defined by the milk industry, while they cooked their meals on stoves heated by wood. Rotary phones connected to party lines. Bathrooms were just off the kitchen so that heat from the wood stove could warm the room.

A key concept to *Purple Trees* concerns broken ties within the family. Many issues can contribute to this, such as death or divorce. I wanted to explore family love in the case of a woman who survived a childhood trauma so great that it subsequently affected her relationship with her children.

While *Purple Trees* centers on Lily Phelps as a distressed woman struggling with a past that twists her perceptions, the story is also about love, family, neighbors, self-sufficiency, and coping with things we cannot control. Lily, in her unique way, excels at coping.

Even though she has many secrets, Lily shows us many truths. The greatest and most touching, is the ability of children to put the needs of others first.

Lily is a figment of my imagination, as are Will, the kids, Belle, Ed, and everyone else in the novel. Willow Springs and Four Rivers are imaginary towns. Lily's past is hers alone.

I hope you enjoyed the story.

ABOUT THE AUTHOR

Ursula Wong writes gripping stories about strong women who struggle against impossible odds to achieve their dreams. Her work has appeared in *Everyday Fiction, Spinetingler Magazine, Mystery Reader's Journal,* and the *Insanity Tales* anthologies. She is a professional speaker appearing regularly on TV and radio.

Wong's debut novel, *Purple Trees,* the enchanting Peruvian folk tale, *The Baby Who Fell From the Sky,* and *Finding My Father: A Story of Vietnam* are available on Amazon and other online retailers.

Her World War II thriller *Amber Wolf,* the first in the Amber War series, is about a young Lithuanian woman who joins resistance fighters. *Amber War,* the second in the series, tells a little-known story of post-World War II Eastern Europe and the continuing fight against the Soviet occupation. *Amber Widow,* third book in the series, matches Eastern European radicals against Russia in a vicious game of nuclear chess. *Black Amber,* fourth book, has cyberterrorists attack the pipeline bringing natural gas from Russia into Germany. In *Gypsy Amber,* fifth book, Russia unleashes a devious plot to thwart China's territorial expansion into Central Asia.

Connect Online:
Website: http://ursulawong.wordpress.com
Email: urslwng@gmail.com

Books by Ursula Wong

Amber Wolf (The Amber War Series Book 1)

Amber War (The Amber War Series Book 2)

Amber Widow (The Amber War Series Book 3)

Black Amber (The Amber War Series Book 4)

Gypsy Amber (The Amber War Series Book 5)

Purple Trees

The Baby Who Fell From the Sky

Finding My Father: A Story of Vietnam

Ursula is available for speaking events and lectures on writing and publishing. For more information, contact her at urslwng@gmail.com and sign up for her popular Reaching Readers newsletter at http://ursulawong.wordpress.com. Finally, reviews are harder to get than you might think. If you were moved by the story, please consider leaving a review on Amazon or sending Ursula email with your thoughts.

Read on for the explosive first chapter of Ursula Wong's novel, *Amber Wolf*

Ludmelia Kudirka is running for her life.

When the brutal Russian soldiers invade 1940's Lithuania, they ravage the countryside and the people. After her mother is murdered, young Ludmelia flees to the safety of the forest. Vowing vengeance, she joins the partisans fighting for freedom in a David-and-Goliath struggle against the mighty Soviet war machine.

A Russian officer ordered to crush the partisans becomes enraged by Ludmelia's escape. Marshalling his killer instincts, he pursues Ludmelia and her fellow warriors into the dark forest, where he has the fight of his life.

Chapter 1

Ludmelia Kudirka lay folded into an awkward shape on the floor of the cramped attic, her long legs aching from their unnatural position. She strained to hear anything from below. Mama was in the kitchen, in her housedress and babushka, probably looking down, as she often did. She had always said if you hide your face, people might forget who you are.

Ludmelia heard the bang of the door slamming against the wall, and then the clump of heavy steps.

"Where is your husband?" The voice was mellow, with a seductive but commanding tone. Ludmelia was astounded at its beauty.

"Dead," said Mama. Her voice sounded calm, betraying no fear.

"Who else lives here?" The second soldier sounded high and sharp, like a rooster.

"No one."

The rooster crowed again. "Don't lie to us woman. Where is your daughter?"

"In the city visiting relatives."

"When did she leave?"

"A few days ago."

"When will she be back?"

"A few days." Ludmelia could almost see her mother shrug.

The clump of steps echoed again. Ludmelia had seen soldiers in 1941, when the Soviets came to Lithuania, and then the Germans. Her Papa had fought the invaders, and Ludmelia and her mother didn't know whether he was alive or dead. They had fled to the countryside, to a little cottage tucked away behind a cluster of trees, where they thought no one would ever find them.

A glass crashed to the floor: it must be the vase in the bedroom where Mama kept wildflowers in the summer. The steps got louder. Would they notice the small door in the corner of the kitchen ceiling? She wanted to climb down and be with Mama. It would be easier to be brave if she was standing in the kitchen next to Mama.

Ludmelia froze at the sound of the mellow voice. "There's no one here. Drive me back to town. You two stay and finish it. We'll come back later for the girl."

A door slammed. There were steps, the scrape of chair legs against the floor, and then the sound of an engine fading in the distance.

"Get us something to eat, old woman," said a raspy voice that sounded like a sleigh sliding over gravel.

Ludmelia heard a shuffling sound. Mama didn't quite lift her feet when she walked, always creating a cloud of dust around her ankles whenever she strode along the road.

"Why do you shuffle your feet, Mama?" Ludmelia had asked one day as they headed to the Rivas farm where Mama cleaned house in exchange for eggs and milk. Ludmelia had held a bouquet of wild flowers for Mrs. Rivas.

"I'm saving my energy."

There was the sound of spoons clanging on the table.

"And something to drink," said the raspy voice.

The shuffling steps crossed the floor to the counter and the jug of *shamarlakas*. They had distilled the moonshine from sugar, and were saving it for winter, when a little drink warmed them quickly. Spoons clanged against plates and slurping sounds drifted into the attic. Ludmelia smelled the stew Mama had made for supper and her stomach growled.

"Leave the jug on the table, woman," said the rooster's voice.

"We're going to have a good time tonight," said the raspy voice.

Before the soldiers came, Ludmelia had been home working, as usual. She had been pacing the floor in the kitchen while darning a sock as the light of the day faded. She was stuck in the countryside with Mama, when she should be studying at University.

"There is no University. The Nazis closed them all," said Mama.

"It's boring here. I never have any fun. I have no friends. We never see anyone."

"I teach you everything you need to know to live. You should be glad."

"I wish I had never been born."

Then two trucks approached the cottage. But no one visited them. Ever.

"They found us."

"Who, Mama?"

"The Bolsheviks." Mama sprang to her feet with energy Ludmelia had never seen before. Mama put a chair under the door to the attic.

"Climb up quickly," said Mama.

"You too, Mama," Ludmelia said as Mama pushed her through the opening.

Mama looked at Ludmelia with eyes that demanded obedience. "Survive for me, Ludie."

Then Mama shut the door.

The space where Ludmelia hid was so small, she couldn't stand or sit, so she lay on her stomach. She pictured the soldiers eating at the kitchen table, and Mama standing near the stove with her hands on her hips.

"Get on the bed," said the rooster's voice.

"You go first, Uri," said the raspy voice.

"No, you."

Ludmelia heard the squeak of the springs in the bed in the corner of the kitchen where she slept, and then Mama's gasp. Ludmelia couldn't bear to think about what they were doing. She pictured herself leaping down, grabbing the butcher knife, and slitting the throats of the soldiers. Blood would wash the floor. She could almost smell the blood. She and Mama would cross Pauksmis Lake, and hide in the old part of the forest where wolves howled in the night. Mama knew places where they would be safe.

Soon the creaking stopped, and Ludmelia heard a soldier grunt. She dug her fingernails into the palms of her hands. Then there was the squeak of the bedsprings again. Ludmelia put her hands over her ears to stop the sound, but the squeak of the springs stung like angry bees.

There was quiet, and then the sound of pottery banging against the table.

"More stew," said the rooster.

"That farmhouse today burned like tinder," laughed the raspy voice.

"Anton, I never expected the old man to run at us with a pitchfork. He's better off dead. The woman, too. They wouldn't have been able to survive the winter with everything burned."

"They were old and had lived their lives. It was no great loss."

The soldiers laughed, and Ludmelia cursed them under her breath. As they talked, she focused on their voices, memorizing every nuance, every intonation. She would never forget those voices, or the names Anton and Uri. She silently repeated the names until they became one hated name tattooed in her memory. The first voice, the beautiful one with no name, was another she couldn't forget, for it had commanded the others to 'finish it.'

The bed squeaked again. The jug of *shamarlakas* thumped against the table. The soldiers grunted, but no sounds came from Mama.

Ludmelia had to pee. She pumped the muscles in her pelvis, desperately trying to quell the need to relieve herself. She pictured pee falling from the cracks in the ceiling onto the heads of the soldiers. How surprised they would be when pee fell into their *shamarlakas*. They would shout up to her, "Come down, Ludmelia." Then they would shoot her for peeing on them. She couldn't pee, for she had to survive. She pumped her muscles until the urge went away.

"Get up," said the raspy voice.

Steps clumped against the floor and the door squeaked.

A gunshot exploded.

Ludmelia bit the back of her hand to stifle her scream. She heard the sound of an engine, and then the sound got soft and disappeared. She opened the door in the ceiling a crack, and peeked down. She couldn't see anyone, just Mama on the bed, covered with the patchwork quilt. Ludmelia opened the door and lowered herself so she was hanging by her fingers. She dropped to the floor like a cat.

The trucks were gone. She ran to the bed. Mama's eyes were closed. "Mama, wake up."

Ludmelia drew back the quilt as a bloom of red formed on Mama's chest. She put her hand on the red, pressing down, trying to stop the blood from flowing. As she willed her strength to pass from her hands into Mama, the old woman sighed, and something changed. Mama became paler and more still. Ludmelia pulled her hand back, suddenly frightened of Mama, whose face had become the symbol of death.

www.ingramcontent.com/pod-product-compliance
Lightning Source LLC
Chambersburg PA
CBHW060806120626
46557CB00001B/102